# MESSENGER PIGEONS

# MESSENGER PIGEONS

Luis Harss

**To order additional copies of this book, please contact:**
Palibrio
1663 Liberty Drive
Suite 200
Bloomington, IN 47403
Toll Free from the U.S.A 877.407.5847
Toll Free from Mexico 01.800.288.2243
Toll Free from Spain 900.866.949
From other International locations +1.812.671.9757
Fax: 01.812.355.1576
orders@palibrio.com
406774

Papa had big hopes. We were going somewhere. We stopped in places for a few days and left. Some job had fallen through. Or he'd caught sight of something else. Always on the move. I was born that way, Mama told me. Bumping along in the back of a truck. Packed in with a crowd. People jumping on and falling off. Field hands, market women with their bundles and baskets. Everyone helped out, tugging at me, wondering if I was a boy or a girl. A rickety little thing, all shaken up, bones sticking out everywhere, the way I'd always be, you could tell, but they made a lot of me: a good-luck baby born on the road. And they loved Mama, who was still almost a kid but already a breasty beauty. They watched her give me her milky warmth. Everyone wanted some of it. It was still a joke months later, when I was too old to be nursing, I should have been running around with the other kids, but I wouldn't let go. Rattling along in some creaky truck or motor cart, sharing food and bench space, they laughed at the way I clung to Mom, and at our strange talk. It sounded like another language to them, though it was just our way of speaking. They drank and sang rancheras. Some had mouth instruments and made music through their teeth, and Papa, craning overboard, blew on a high-pitched bone pipe he pulled out of his cape, his spirit whistle.

That was our life. In carts, trucks, open buses. Hanging on to each other. Up dusty hot roads. Long distances sometimes. No family or friends anywhere. All dead or gone, nothing left of them but what was in our bones, I'd heard Papa say. Wrapped in his cape, we got off with our bundle wherever there was work. Market towns that needed jobbers, street sweepers, ditch and dam diggers. Sweaty temporary jobs for big men, earth movers. And Papa was always the first to get hired, he stood out right away in line, a commanding presence, head and shoulders above everyone else, with his tall bony frame, a proud man who knew his true worth, even when his clothes hung in rags from him. He could do anything, drag a cart like a horse, rip out trees, drive earth-clawing machinery, bury mounds of garbage, dig a hole for a well, practically with his bare hands, or strapped into a harness, shoulder any weight, bring down a wall, nothing stopped him. Night and day, even without food or sleep, reaching out beyond himself.

Meantime, Mama went off with the market women. Flower girls and basket women who after dark became night ladies, in gaudy make-up and bursting out of their busty clothes. We'd rent part of a shed and wait and they'd call for her. They fixed her up by candlelight before a cracked mirror. Lavished soaps, powders, colors, sprays on her, patted her into her pretty shape. She was shy the first times. But soon she did it all herself. Just a sprinkle of scent, it was all she needed. Wearing her own face, it showed through her painted mask, and any rough dress she could slip out of easily. I almost couldn't watch, she was so beautiful, it made me cry. And she held me, for a long time, before going. She had to tear herself away. She left me on a bedroll, in the care of some old granny grouch, looking in on me every few minutes. I'd hear her laughing and singing outside. Then she'd be gone for awhile and she'd come back with money stuffed in her bust. I'd been aching for her, but glad she was making people happy. They were steamy nights and she moved in a glow: a kind of bloom she gave out when she worked. Like when we bathed together in a foamy river, our skins dull and dusty when we went in, and came out shining. And sometimes people came to see me in candlelight, from around the market, and others who slept on pallets in corners of the shed, they touched and poked me. I'd crawl into a body-shaped hole I'd made for myself in the dirt floor. Mama had taught me to do that. They prayed and fussed over me, called me a blessed angel and other names. Then Mama would be back and she'd sing her bird song into my ear. Quietly, under her breath, when my bones ached, just a sort of warbling in her chest and throat. It was about two blind birds. One, blinded by life, sang its sorrow. The other one, born blind, saw in the dark, and sang its joy. I wasn't sure what the song meant, except that it was about us.

Papa would be out there, doing night work, for extra pay, or because he hadn't found anything else, but we felt his cape around us, as if he'd left it behind, with his shape in it.

Sometimes he was gone for days, answering some call, we thought we'd never see him again, off in his other world. But he made his way back, bringing presents, things he'd found or bought, bones for whistles, maybe a sunstone, a human-shaped root, or some toy he'd invented, a puppet on a string, to show me a new exercise he'd devised for me, birds he made out of newspaper. Always watching over us, from wherever he was.

Once we landed in jail with several ladies. It could happen at any time because of some law against us. A place called Rosales, with sunny streets, walls overgrown with desert roses. We'd borrowed a parasol and had a nice walk in the afternoon. I was up as long as I'd ever been on my spindly legs. At night we joined the ladies. There was some fun, music, animal ghost figures, a lamplit courtyard. A police wagon took us in, dumped us, overnight, in an underground cell, with drunks and beggars besides the ladies, a black stinkhole. And Papa came for us, in the middle of the night. He'd been moonlighting, and seeing things. Gesturing when they asked him who he was, as he always did, trying to make himself understood. Bully cops shoved him down the steps into our hole. He didn't resist: he'd planned it all, to be with us. We whispered in the dark, under his cape, which had sleeves and pockets no one could have imagined, so they'd let him keep it. Voices made loud sound waves down there, but no one heard us, gathered into ourselves. Hours went by. We heard people crying, tossing in bad dreams, curled up or out cold on the hard floor. By morning it was still dark, but Papa made an eyehole in the air with two fingers so I could look out into the light. You paid to be let go and people waited at the gate for their families, but Papa handed money out of a secret pocket, and we were on our way.

In another town, while Mama was with the ladies, or doing herself up in a beauty shop, he took me around, showing me things. It was one of those days when I could barely hold myself up, all disjointed, my bones snapping like dry twigs, so he carried me, on his shoulders, up a slope to where there was a view, from a ledge, over a valley in a deep haze, a great inspiring sight, on display for me, arranged by his powerful magic. We'd caught a donkey cart out, but it broke a wheel halfway. So he scooped me up off my legs and climbed on foot with me strapped to his back. We followed a craggy, rough path, hard on my sore joints, even fitting myself into his body. We heard bird calls in thorn trees, cave-like echoes. The trail led up to a blinding light, hot as a bush fire. He went sliding and scraping, sometimes on hands and knees. I hung on, with every bone. The sun striking the rocks gave off flintstone sparks. The desert heat crackled like lit matches, rubble rolling back down the slope behind us. We snagged on cactus spikes. I was burning up in the blaze, I pulled a flap of the cape up over my head. We breasted a boulder and reached the lookout point, high up, on the ledge. From there, stretching into space with his spirit whistle, Papa made a call, then threw out his arms, waving at some birds that were flying in circles overhead like vultures, I thought they were, and that they'd swoop down and pluck out my eyes, but he said they were messenger pigeons. A feathery storm out there, with black wings, like flying ashes. With a sweep of his arms that somehow drew them in, he brought them down toward us and waved them up and away again, into the sky, blowing on the whistle, which was so high-pitched that I couldn't hear it, though it throbbed in my ears. He was listening, too, hovering over the depths, as if tuning into the world, and I clung to him tooth and claw as we set off a landslide of loose stones climbing back down the slope.

We moved on, to other towns. Drawn by some sight or sound, churchbells, fireworks, a music band, wherever we landed when our transport dropped us off by the road. Maybe just a little prickly cactus town but with a walk and a fountain of papery water. And there'd be work for strong arms, and night life. We'd rent a shed for the night, pay up in the morning and go. We traveled light, with just our clothes bundle, which was also my bed bag, mama's toiletries, and the sling I slept in when my straps weren't enough to hold me together. There was always something going on: sales, fairs, parades. Whatever the occasion, it meant jobs, fiesta nights. And wonders, everywhere. Papa came and went, sprained his back all day at some construction job, meantime thinking up new things, then making them happen. He'd hear voices in a well, see distant places nearby, upside down buildings in a reflecting pond. Big things no one understood. And little ones, for small change. Tricks he had for kids and grown-ups. Rags and whistles he pulled out of his sleeves, shredded papers like whispery flames, fidgety beings he made from wires and bits of string.

If shadows of wings beat in a tree, he'd wave and bring pigeons down on his head and shoulders.

I was with Mama in our shed, or in some arbor, under a thatch roof. By the road, maybe near a creek where we could splash and cool off. She got me cleaned up, freed of my straps and bindings for awhile, put me through some walking steps, light as air. Or we'd wrap around each other, just being close, as evening fell. Shivery even on the hottest nights from not having eaten all day. Soon the love ladies came by. They'd been in touch somehow, or knew about us, and treated us like family. Pretty flower girls in their lacy blouses, and old bags painted up to make their wrinkles look like kindly frowns and smiles. A noisy flock busying up for the night. They were kissy women with a fleshy warmth. Their shiny images clouded in the cracked make-up mirror, lit by a dim bulb with moths flickering around it, they drank pissy drinks, beauty potions, boiled herbs against disease, dabbing on their night faces, scented and powdered on attractive colors. Fanning themselves, in feather ruffs, padded rumps and falsies. They chatted and prayed, sobbed with loud gasps when they were unhappy, and sniffed things in their hankies. They all had troubles and sobbed and suffered. On their knees for a minute before they went out, gazing at the frail cross of light in the bare bulb. They were great believers. Some with smiling masks and eyelashes like wax dolls. Popping out of their bodices and girdles, sweaty in the heat that seemed to steam out of some deep cooking pit smoldering under us. They clucked over me, kissed my eyes and ears, sloppy wet kisses, felt me all over, as if they saw something in me, listening to my parroty talk, which was what my chatter sounded like. They wanted to bring some wise man to look at me. Once a lady with bright pupils—she wore tiny glasses inside her eyes— said she'd seen me in a dream. She lit a candle for me. Mama said it was because of my inner beauty. They sprinkled scents on me, glitter to make me shine. A Maria, as she was known, wanted to show me off at the fair, where kids posed for pictures. She had me try on a frilly body net. I got all tangled in it. Some just cried their hearts out over me. And I squatted and left a puddle, as I'd seen them do in the bushes, then curled up with my bones in my body-shaped hole.

Then Mama was gone with someone, in her bosomy top, she was a big success. Drinking, laughing, having girlish fun. I'd hear skirts swishing, up and down the footpaths, bugs sizzling in the firelight. And she'd be back, shivering in the early morning chill, hiding some bruise, or a cigarette burn, and we'd lie there together, dug into our hole in the earth, and she'd sing her bird song to me. She breathed her breath into me when I wasn't well, fed me with her tongue, straight out of her mouth. Sometimes she could still make milk for me, when I was crying in her arms like a baby. We felt Papa's shape around us, from wherever he was, out working overtime, thinking of us.

I led my own life, when I was well enough, some days. And when we stayed longer in one place. Maybe in a shack with a yard where I could play. I'd scramble around after the market kids. On elbows and knees at first, a crabby crawl, it was all I could do. They'd find me in the yard scratching in the dust with chickens pecking at me. I struggled to keep my head up. I drank drainwater or a leak from a tap. A freaky little scarecrow with a beaky nose. Doing my parrot talk, which made people stop and listen. The kids came and stared and threw things at me, while Mama was out. In the daytime, too, she'd be gone for awhile, especially when Papa hadn't been doing so well, leaving me in my sling or caught in a rope hammock, where I couldn't fall out, even with my twitchy movements, and a granny supposedly watching over me, but the kids would rush in, swing me up high, dump me on the ground and run off. Other times I just hung there, smelling the river vapors. Breathing them in and coming alive. My whole body stirring. My hair growing wild or shaved off, once when I had lice. While the granny dozed, somehow I'd work myself free and go wallow in a puddle. I could roll over and kick out my legs. I ate dirt and chicken feed and licked plaster off the walls, and flapped my rags at neighbors who looked in. In time, I got around, wearing the thong harness Papa had made for me. Strapped up under my arms and between my legs, in short flights, like a bumble bug, I wandered among vegetable stands and cooking fires, climbed over crates, stole scraps of food, hid behind clothing racks, strings of peppers and sausages. Primped up in my straps, for all to see. People would let me by to get rid of me, or send me on some dumb errand, as a joke. Someone would give me a stick for a crutch, or throw me into the air and catch me. Or they'd let me taste something, try on a fiesta costume, cure-all charms and bracelets, or hug a prayer doll that could make me well. There were all sorts of things, bodies to get into, as a witchy lady told me. Dozens of food and medicine stands, piles of pretty trinkets, toothy combs, eyeglasses through which you saw things change shapes and colors. I had a begging act, getting into a contortion, like a dwarf I'd seen who stood on his head extending a foot instead of his hand. A music band blew trumpets to announce me. They shoved me along, shooed me off. Stray animals trailed me, sniffing at me. I'd lose my footing and roll over a barrel. Billboard signs lit up, bristling hot drinks and charcoal fires. I got things going, like Papa. And it all got into me. In one place a neon head with pins stuck in it flashed on and off when it saw me coming. It was a headache ad with a face that split open in a welcoming smile. A shade cloth rippled overhead, mixing light and shadow, striped tarps made waves. People burned incense for saints, smokes behind bead curtains. Kids lit sparklers and candy skulls on sticks. They chased after me wearing burro hats and cowheads. And I ambled around, broken up but burning to live. It was like a fever boiling over in me. Saints in tin chapels followed me with their eyes. Rag dolls hanging from hooks in dollhouses threw their arms around my neck. I drank honey water, which was like sour curds, and a cactus drink, and coconut milk, which made your skin glow, and chewed on a holy weed against bone pain. Everything had some power, I knew that from Papa, you just had to tap into it. And they wanted to do something for me. Squatting herb women who fanned me with their skirts. Healers trying to grab hold of me: manazas, big hands, who molded bodies like clay. Another man carved angels and aged them with a blowtorch. They said he made souls out of bodies. I'd get away somehow. A wind would blow me along. Awnings whipped over my head. Papers and dead leaves flitted about and stuck to me. Garbage birds flew down on me from the trees. And I made faces and got people to pick me up and carry me on their shoulders, from where I had a view, breathing in smokes and smells. Bicycle carts and motor carts that went by gave me rides. And someone would catch me by the hair and dangle me, flapping my arms and legs, like a jumping jack on pullstrings. There was a man with talking birds who tried to get me into a conversation with them. Almada, the birdman: I saw him in several places. He also had songbirds in cages, under a hood, and he'd rip off the hood and the bird would gush and warble. Other birds, uncaged, perched on clothes hangers, didn't need a hood, they'd just start singing and couldn't stop and wouldn't fly away. I'd heard he blinded them so they'd sing on and on. Sometimes he wore feathers and claws and watched me through a mask with a beak. I made friends with donkeys: they'd let me climb, off a crate, onto the dip in their backs, and carry me waddling on crooked legs. And paper dragons in puppet dances batted wings at me. Ladies would call me from behind folding screens. They painted beauty spots on me. They said having me around brought them customers. Then the kids would drag me around like a toy on wheels, they'd tie me to a scooter and jerk me along or walk me by the legs on my hands, like a wheelbarrow, through mazes of hanging things, skins, guts, plucked birds, strips of meat, chewing gum figures, string cheese, sausages and beads, necklaces like nooses. Girls dressed and undressed me like a doll and had me talk my parrot talk. I could smoke like a bat and drink from a skull. The birdman once almost trapped me under a hood. Another time, mocking Papa, a gang caught a pigeon and slit its crop open looking for its message. They dangled me half-naked over a cooking pot, where I did a boy-girl act, with my two baby balls, sucking them up into their hollows and letting them droop in their sack again. And then, in a fair, I played a miracle child. I'd seen one showing off, in fancy embroidery, on a starry throne, wearing a wreath, in a chapel made of upended crates, people pinning wishes on him, tin arms and legs, a bleeding heart, and the kids hoisted me up on a toilet seat in a hutch and shot bottle caps at me, and I rolled off into the dirt, licking myself in parts of the body nobody else could reach.

We'd set out whenever we could get a lift. In a night bus, a delivery truck, with road workers, families in carts, anything Papa could summon out of the dark, walking along the edge of the road, as traffic swept by, sooner or later they'd pick us up, they knew we were somebody. We crowded in with bags and animals. They always made room for us, many times wouldn't even take our money. Travelers and market-goers. On long distance buses that slowed but didn't stop for you, and locals, chugging along lopsided. People hanging off roof racks, kids riding bumpers. All headed somewhere they needed to be: a job, a shrine, a hospital. Able hands out of work, hot and sick people, we heard a lot of stories, when they got into conversation, driven from their homes, or just looking for a better place to live, packed into carts with their belongings, furniture and housewares, on the move like us. There'd be some backcountry people with a sense of direction even at night. And Papa, looking into the next day, predicted the weather, from sightings of birds and clouds.

Mama was carrying a new baby: it showed in her bloom of wellbeing, though she'd just started it, you could barely hear its rumor, if you put your ear up close, but after drying up for several months she was making milk again, I'd been tasting it, and it was sweet as honey.

Once we landed in a town plaza. On a sunny holiday. Everything floated in heat waves. Mama spread out her parasol with rainbow streaks. Papa had made it for her with a cane and lightweight wrapping that folded in on ribs like toothpicks. He gave out paper pigeons to the kids. They caught the breeze, then evening shadows. The police questioned us but let us go. Not like other times when they'd run us in for sleeping in the street. At nightfall the plaza lit up. Lamps and trees with strands of lights. People strolling by. They came for the spectacle. Vendors and performers. Ladies in chatty groups. A fountain threw out a cool spray, a pony wheel whirled, playing loudspeaker music, kids strapped to the shaggy horses with bushy taills. They let me ride for free, round and round, in the dip of a sway back. A kid shared my mount, feeling my bones from behind. Papa swept around in his cape, pulling riches out of his rags, blowing bird whistles. And Mama went and stood up in the bandstand, in her airy dress, under the flared canopy, which was like a bigger parasol, and everyone could tell she was a love lady.

Soon after, a roadshow picked us up. They had a box stage on wheels, yoked to a hooded ox. They were playing mysteries, a Holy Family, shepherds following a star, wanderers on a stormy night, with music and sound effects, and I rode a noisemaker Papa built for them in their workshop, driven by a bicycle chain. It took his weight on the pedals to get it started, but then I was freewheeling. A foil caught the wind and flapped to make thunder. A weathervane spun and a goose horn honked. I let loose with everything. And he took over from a music man, got into a contraption the man was wearing and beat drums and cymbals, rubbed on a washboard, and wailed over several harmonicas mounted on a rack attached to a battered guitar, all at once.

Days later we were on a float. It was a flower festival. A poor town with only a few trees, but petals raining like sunflakes. Some garlanded ladies on a buckboard pulled Mama up with me into their cloud of blossoms. Papa joined a mariachi band, playing a pipe. Dancers worked up an excitement. I got some steps in and kept my balance. Kids leapfrogged over me, and I jumped after them, kicking out my legs, my heart pounding, however I landed. And I was still in a fever at night. I walked around in my mind, as I did sometimes. Papa saw me writhing in my sling. Mama lulling and hushing me. He took us out to the fair, where he made lightning for me, flashes of matches between his fingers. He didn't even need matches, he could snap his nails and spark a fire. He had some whistles to sell, and string puppets. In minutes kids were climbing all over him. We'd left Mama at a beauty stand, trying on wigs displayed on bare heads. Flowers were still falling. Wilted petals, slippery underfoot. We were caught in a commotion. There'd been an accident, a man lay torn up on the ground, and they needed me to stop the blood, with the freaky power some people thought I had. And there were games for kids and disguises, laughing masks, and an x-ray machine where you stuck a hand or a foot in a slot and saw your bones. I imagined I saw my whole skeleton with everything in its right place, a sort of twin living inside me, my real self, doing all the things I couldn't do, as it did in dreams sometimes, getting me up and out of myself, once I'd even sleepwalked and wandered, light and free, on to the road, a lady had brought me back.

Wherever we stopped there were ladies. As soon as we found a place to stay, while Papa was off on a night job, they came for Mama. She was beautiful and happy, with her milky glow, brimming over when she laughed and sang. Out in the night lights, everyone wanted her. And they liked having me around, dressing me up in girl or boy things, hanging jewels or charms on me, or just resting a hand on me for a moment. Different ladies I got to know. Done up for holidays and parties. Some were mourners who wept in wakes. Others were wetnurses who made their own babies to keep their milk flowing. They grew huge dugs like udders. We met one with four breasts. She said they were just part of the job. And some carried babies for other women. Matchmakers made the arrangements. Busybody businesswomen. And nuns gave unwanted babies away. Sometimes they were ladies dressed as nuns, dangling crucifixes and prayer beads. One of them blessed me one day with a little bone she kept in a powder box. She said it was a relic and she could say mass with it, and that the puff pads in the box were communion wafers. She wore a headdress, and another time I saw her with a big hair-do. They were all themselves and other selves when they went out in their sumptuous gowns with pop-up corsets and feather fans. They drank firewaters and performed in sheds. I helped them hang on outfits meant to drop off and leave them in thongs and pin-prick jewelry. They stashed bills in their garter belts. Some wore straps, like my harness, and changed shapes in them. People stuck pasties on them like wishes on saints. They showed me moves, twisting out of their clothes the way I imagined slipping out of my skin. One told me that stripping felt like you were getting into another body. It sounded like me in my dreams. Days when I was so stiff in my creaky bones that Mama had to walk me along stepping on her toes. But pretty in my light dress, she said, and she held me up, stretching out of myself, to kiss my reflection in a window.

We had some hard times, looking for work. Places where we weren't wanted. Or Papa got into a temper and walked out. Even when we'd been doing well, Mama making a good living, we wanted something more. Papa always aiming high, watching for an opportunity. Once he carried billboard ads around a town. Way up there, on stilts, over the smoke and noise, like a saints' day giant. He could have been a glassblower or a fireeater, or one of those underground spirits that caused earthquakes. He unloaded trucks on night shifts, carted crates and carcasses, whatever he could get his hands on, bellowing with pent-up force. Then, waking me out of my wraps, he'd take me sightseeing. Spitting out some boiling drink he said was good for me, we'd pick our way through fire lights, the wheezy breaths of sleepers and low voices, listening for invisible bugs, which kept the market alive at night, and other calls and signals, birds that stirred in dark branches, or loose animals that came when he spoke to them in our way.

Sometimes we went on visits, with Mama. Just to let ourselves be seen, she said. She had a moonlit glow those days. It was the happiness of making her baby. I'd drunk some brew that kept me awake. Night ladies took us in. Love ladies and others who read palms or gave advice. They went through their motions with me, fanned me with a palm frond or patted a beauty face on me, like one of those masks they wore against wrinkles. There was still a crackling atmosphere after a hot day. Once a red sky split through black clouds and cinders blew about like fireflies. Papa said it was a volcano in the distance. It lit us up all night. We'd just arrived in that town and didn't have a place to sleep. Other times someone else had moved into our place while we were out. Or we'd been threatened and we couldn't go back. So we wandered, looking around. People gave us directions, waving to drive us off. They'd be waiting for us but duck behind a curtain when they saw us. Flower girls emptied sink water on us. A prowler would flash a blade at us but let us by. Once Papa had had his face slashed with a razor, but it didn't show until the next day. A mist rose where the ground had been hosed down.

Sometimes a damp breath from a river draining sewage. The market gathered up, tarps and stands folding. The garbage birds flapped down. We heard chants and shuffling steps. Bums raked through the trash. People lay sprawled on pallets, straw mats, mesh hammocks, airing out in the breeze. Animals roamed, rubbing up against us. They'd hang around being friendly, then one would try to drag me off. Monster animals, too, ghost paper dragons with bat wings. Devils with clacking jaws from some dentist's shop. Charcoal fires smoked out, scattering ashes like black petals. The ground still hot as embers, it burned through our rope sandals. Bodies and souls flaming. Whatever it was Papa saw. After a rain there'd be frogs croaking. Born in the puddles, some mewed like cats. We'd find a shelter and bundle up in our body-shaped hole. Sometimes we could rent a foam rubber mattress. Mama said we had to get our beauty sleep so we'd look our best the next day. I listened to the heartbeats in her belly. And soon Papa would be up and around. He'd heard pigeons cooing somewhere. He could be out walking till dawn. We thought he'd been taken away. Mama would go out asking for him. And stray animals would come and breath on me. I'd wake up in the middle of the night and there'd be some creature chewing on my hair or licking my face. Once it was a night lady with a superstition sticking a pin in me.

I still got around on my own. Hitching rides, or with my sleepwalking steps. Along a ditch or an alley. I had my grab holds and places to stop. Cookeries where I'd snatch a bite to eat: fritters or a scoop of chocolate meat or beans. Women called me from booths. Healers who wanted to get at me. They hung lockets on me, gave me drinks that burned through my veins. Once there was a midwife. She did births and washouts. She had me hug a doll that was me. It was made of real bones and a skull with real hair and teeth, by bush people, who came in to buy matches and salt or soap. And Almada the birdman was always around, or someone like him, with the talking birds and the songbirds that never stopped, swaying on a clotheshanger or flapping in the air at the end of a string. Once I saw him stick a needle through a bird's eye. A little fluttery warbler that let out a big burst of song. I felt it as if it was coming out of me. He tried to throw a hood over my head. And then I was being jerked along by the market kids, on a leash or in a handcart. Messenger kids, shoeshines, photo kids. They did shows with me where I was a doll or a slave, or a girl pretending to be a boy. They squeezed parroty sounds out of me. And sometimes they let me into their gangs. We stole things, passing them along, down the line, smoked butts made of twigs and bug legs. I couldn't keep up but was good at twisting in and out of places. I forgot I wasn't one of them. In a livestock market we had a nanny goat that gave cheesy milk, and wool, and let itself be mounted like a woman. We kicked a skin ball around and drank from a bladder. But then they'd roll me head over heels and I'd be myself again. There were some strange kids: baby girls nursing babies, little old kids with wrinkles, idiot kids people kept as pets, but I was something else, I knew it when a stand set food out for me or I felt one of those tin saints following me with his eyes. Once I fell into the hands of a badman called Bandera. He trained kids as beggars, taught them to act dumb or crippled. He could turn boys into girls. He said he gave them many lives. You saw them walking on stumps or crutches. There was a rumor he really broke their bones. He was deformed like them, a bearded dwarf. He called me, up an alley, when he saw me, sat me on a barber's chair, spun me around to have a good look at me, and I was expecting him to work some kind of a change in me, but he told me I didn't need anything more, I'd always be noticed, just as I was.

In a flag-happy town there was a pageant. Crowds streaming in, villagers and horsemen doing paces. Everyone in fiery colors. We'd seen flowering crosses along the road on our way in. We rode on a jangling cart with a puppet show. They had stick figures that did stunts, flips and handstands, and bobbing heads on strings. Papa knew some finger movements. They let him do a wire dancer. Then he made animal shadows with his hands. And he lit sparks that opened cracks in the air. Later, in the parade, he was a sandwichboard man. The stores were having big sales. The paraders carried laughing faces on candy sticks like lollipops, jumping jacks with flap arms and legs. There were loudspeakers, trumpet bands, churchbells, feather dancers beating skin drums. Firecrackers went off like flying souls, broomstick rockets like witches, birds winging out of bonfires. Some were Papa's pigeons, mixed in with the garbage birds. He was doing winged shapes, working on something. A way out, Mama said, into a world his size. That vaster and deeper world he'd come from. I wandered with her in fiesta colors.

She had her baby glow. I wore piñata paper shreds and fringes. Breezes with streamers blew us about. I made people laugh with my antics and parrot talk. They tossed me coins and bottle tops. We lit a wick in fat at a faith shop. In back was the smokehouse where they scorched and blanched relics. In another shed they boiled skulls. You saw the brains melting out. Mama got into an argument with some joy ladies. They weren't the ones we knew. She was attracting too much attention. They wanted us to move on. But soon they were all hugging and kissing. I ran off with some kids who slit a pig's throat and drank its blood. They didn't like my looks and they bundled me up and lowered me down a well in a bucket. I went banging down, bouncing against the sides, into a shithole at the bottom, and they spat and pissed on me, but I wasn't afraid, because with my loose joints I could climb places where others couldn't, and as soon as they were gone I worked my way up a metal ladder, over the rim, and washed at a pump, where ladies splashed water on me.

We rode out on a donkey. A stray Papa had caught in a ridge outside town. They lived there like mountain goats in the rocks. Runaway donkeys that had gone wild, they couldn't be broken. That was what people said. But he talked to it, roped it and brought it in. He got it buckled and fancied up. Spent all his money on the trimmings, flaps and saddlebags. It didn't look like much: just a potbellied donkey with a toothy smile, but surefooted as a goat, it could get us anywhere. A prayer man said it was a saintly donkey, because of the way it went down on its knees to let Mama on. He didn't notice Papa flicking a switch.

And it had a birthmark: a bony knob like the stub of a horn on its forehead, from a monster ancestor. We took off, bright in the morning, down the stone road, and in mid-afternoon we were still going, at a steady pace, from town to town, Papa riding with me at times, till donkey's bristly back sagged, then Mama, holding me, Papa striding alongside, under his cape, his long-legged walk. Mama with her parasol. The sun beating down on us, we were something to look at. Even when we couldn't stop, places where they wouldn't let us get off, people came out on the road to watch us go by.

It was a new life. Clomping along a road, between creaky carts and rundown buses, in whirls of dirt, we'd break out into the light. They were beautiful sunny days with just a few patches of clouds like birds drifting on high with outspread wings, our hopes soaring. As if we'd caught a breath that was bigger than us. Wanderers on the open road, into great looming distances. We gave donkey its head, it knew the way. Carried us body and soul, mama said. It was a honky donkey with a gassy belly and a happy hee-haw laugh. Papa led on foot, his cape flapping like a sail, even when there wasn't a wisp of air. In the blinding glare, but he could see. Mama under her blazing parasol. She let me hold the rein. I wore a donkey hat. I had saddle sores from the bumpy ride. But we got through a dust storm and days of white heat, the sun cracking our skulls, we didn't care. Papa was of the air, like his whistles. Mama was of the earth, where I could sleep and wake up. Donkey's hooves gave out flinty sparks. It sounded like a traveling organ with its loud belly music, making flops as it went, calm and self-contained, speeding up when it sensed water nearby, a trickle of a creek or pooled in a ditch. Then, baring its teeth and braying, it went and guzzled. But it barely needed to eat or drink, it had a sort of camel hump Papa discovered where it stored water and it could go on forever, only pulling off now and then to graze on the weeds that grew along the edge of the road, anything it could find, when it had hunger pangs, thatch off a roof, or straw stuffing from a mattress someone had hung out a window. And I had a hold, even when I was alone in the saddle, I could stay on, showing off a bit, I'd straddle it somehow, hugging its scratchy hide, and buck and bump along. Long, sweaty days, till it dropped us off near a roadhouse or a bonfire. Stops where people camped and bathed, in a split in the rocks. There'd be a foamy stream that gurgled like a drain. Sometimes a shed with sleeping mats, a rag bed for me. Maybe a reed screen for privacy, if Mama had a visitor while Papa was doing his rounds. You could buy candles and flatbread. We set donkey loose, never hobbled or tethered it, so it could wander all night in the bush, out of sight, where no one could steal it, and it was back in the morning, all Papa had to do was blow on a donkey whistle and it came trotting, ready to get going. Or, even before we called it, at first light, we'd hear it snort and snuffle in the shadows, a smelly presence, fresh out of a splash in some muddy river or itching with burrs. And we were off, and seeing things. Flights of birds and distant hills. A lake floating in the air, though it hadn't rained for months. a great inland ocean that had once existed, Papa said, you could still see it. We stopped at roadside chapels with saints made of body parts of people killed in traffic accidents, prettied-up skeletons and mummies. The bare-boned road would wind through a canyon like a dry river bed. But we'd follow some procession carrying trees of life. Always something unexpected crossing our path. There'd be a burned-out village still smoking, after a torch-lit fiesta. Graveyards with cactus crosses. And sometimes a graveyard town with hollowed-out houses and streets, people gone looking for work, or driven out by troubles or a disease, a fear that had hit suddenly, and we rode right through, waving off the pigeons. At the next town there was hope again. And somehow we announced our coming. At a quiet time of day. In our cloud of dust. People came out on the road to meet us. They let us off to rest in an arbor, when we stopped for shade at noon or for a bucket of water from a well, a dip in a molten hot river. I'd swing from a tree in my sling. I held on to my bones and my rolling head. They had to help Mama off the donkey with her baby belly. She'd lost the baby one night, but kept its shape. A blessed angel, they called it, like they used to call me. It made us shine in people's eyes. In other places they set dogs on us, tied firecrackers to donkey's tail, or kids ran out to sell us things, we never knew what might happen. At guard posts sometimes they felt us down, with a special body search for Mama and hands all over me, too, laughing at my freaky movements, and we had to pay a tax or a toll to get through. But mostly they treated us with respect, Papa knew how to handle the situation, even when they didn't understand what he said, towering over them in his cape, things falling out of his sleeves, and Mama carrying her baby, though she wasn't anymore. Up on our honky donkey with our dignity, people felt it. Wherever we were going, we'd get there. And at the next place they were expecting us. As if we'd called ahead. They'd ask us in and we'd sit and drink refreshments, cooling off in the late afternoon, or on a lamplit porch at night, gathered with a family, in leafy shadows, just being there, because they wanted us to stay, keeping company, without words. Mama holding me on her belly, Papa emptying his sleeves and pockets of fluttery things on webs and strings, broken shells or bits of pottery, fossils he called them, meaning they'd been buried for centuries, until he'd dug them up somewhere, sparkling stones he'd picked up along the road, and when he threw them away nobody could find them, they crumbled into dust. Kids climbing all over him. Donkey outside the window, in a haystack, made its gassy noises. There might be a musician, and Papa would help him tune, with a tuning fork he made out of some bit of scrap metal, or blowing on a reed flute he'd invented that played a scale. In a dirt farm they milked a cow for us, and the farmer let me drink out of his cupped hands. It was so rich it made me sick. In another house, a woman wanted to breast feed me, because their cow had sore teats and its milk was sour, but she was afraid I'd bite her. I played with the house pets, dogs, cats, chickens, pigs, I got along with them all. We'd linger awhile, Papa doing his tricks to entertain the children, hand shadows, a vanishing act, and they hung on to us, they wouldn't let us go, we had to tear ourselves away.

We passed through poor towns in ruins, just a few threadbare trees left, but there was always someone to take us in. A lady would have a sleep house for transients. Just a hutch where you rented floor space, but with tap water and a meal. We'd meet salesmen, people with music, families waiting for someone to be let out of jail. A night watchman would come by. He'd heard of Papa's whistles. And along the road, where a desert wind blew, in little outlying settlements, there were food shacks with shady spots in back. Some with power stolen from the main line even had an electric fan. Papa could fix it if it was broken. Even in the dark, when there was an outage. He'd work in the moonlight, joining live wires with his bare fingers. Donkey sticking his head in the window hole, breathing on us like a bellows. Gone half the night, but his noise was always with us. On dangerous nights we'd sleep in a ditch. There might be a drunken brawl or shooting gangs. Armed workmen clashed with helmeted troops. We'd see horses go by without riders. We heard of towns emptying, everyone headed for the border. It was the talk, at hiring posts for day laborers, brazos. Papa brought back the news. People who'd been across. They'd found life and work on the other side. And it wasn't just that. A bigger way of doing things, he said. But we had a long way to go. Barren fields stretched between towns. We got caught in broken-down traffic. Off the main road, when we wanted to stay out of sight for a few days, scrawny animals roamed, all bones and horns. At times we beat off swarms of bugs, gnats, flying beetles, monster moths at night, flies without wings that stuck to us like slugs. We

got through some dark storm days. A blinding dust
swirled around us. Donkey had to wear a head bag
or a fly mask. We muffled up in Papa's cape, or a
wrap-around cloth when he was out ahead, finding
a breathing space in the folds, and we put in an
appearance in a town with a lot of wounded people,
and cripples, you almost couldn't tell which was
which. Sleeperies and eateries set up everywhere.
There was a shrine with healing waters nearby.
Humps, goiters, tumors dragged down to the banks
of the river. Stumps of people missing eyes and legs,
all those body parts they stuck on saints in the form
of tin wishes, you could buy hearts, breasts, men's
balls. Big hands, manazas, waited smoking in tents.
They reached out for me as I went by, sprinkling
feathers and ashes on me. Papa took me around to
show me off. Though he said it wasn't my time yet.
They all tried to touch me. A man who sold manikins
wanted to buy me. In another town a crazy lady had
tried to steal me. She'd said I was her lost baby. At
night, in our shed, a smoker dropped embers from his
pipe into my belly button, mixed with spit and leaf
mold. I'd been in pain, squirming and squawking.
It was one of my fevers. Almada the birdman came
in and listened. Papa played a whistle over me, and
people looked in. We kept a wavering candlelight
going. Like shady waters with restless images. I was
dreaming of my real self. Floating in a pond with
all sorts of impossible movements of my arms and
legs. Mama sang her bird song, warbling in my ear.
Donkey was there, too, we hadn't dared set it loose,
its head in a feed bag, to keep it quiet, and a shit bag
behind to catch its flops. And when people stopped

coming, their candle shadows gone, we gathered up and left in a hurry.

We stayed places where there was work. Or in some inviting spot along the road. Between the ramshackle bean and taco shops that had set up with stolen electricity, food carts and moveable kitchens sharing awnings and eaves for shade, alleys that caught cool drafts, we'd rent a shack, fix it up a bit, make it into a home for a few days. We whitewashed the walls, Papa did repairs, we spread some bright colors, straw mats, hung a shawl for decoration, a few streamers, we got bedding, trellises for the windows, to keep out the bugs but let the air through, and we ran a curtain across a back room for privacy. Sometimes there was even an outhouse. And shrubbery nearby for donkey fodder. Maybe a pile of corn husks or a haystack. Neighbor women came in to help. They brought pans and folding chairs and witchy charms, and the smell of cookeries. There was always an electric fan with a turning head, like a wise owl. It blew across a bar of ice, when we could get one from the ice truck. Papa bought or borrowed some kind of permit. We sold drinks and smokes. He left the business to Mama and set off on donkey at a smart clippety clop, his long legs dangling down the sides, almost reaching the ground. He'd be gone all day, at a job or one of his sightings. Places where the earth was moving but only animals sensed it and scattered. He'd follow a twister up a road or find a boneyard with whistle bones, and sit and work on them with the awls and razors he carried in his cape. So far gone in his thoughts we didn't expect him back. While he was away, men came in. All kinds, with their needs, or for fun. Off their carts and trucks. Having heard of us or just passing by. They knew about us in town, too, from the ladies. Mama took them into the back room. She had a cushiony mattress. She lit sweet smokes and market scents, gave them papery powders to breathe. I could see through the thin curtain. Her beauty overflowing, and they worshiped her, kissed her breasts, listened to her baby, as if it were really there. She let them talk or cry, got them out of some rage or nightmare. They told her things they wouldn't have told anyone else. She drank and sang with them. Burned them up with her heat, turning their pains into pleasures. And they spent everything they had on her. One man brought her flowers with the stems in glass tubes, they didn't wilt for days. He'd left a bruise on her the time before, where she already had a shiny scar, like a vaccination mark, from a cigarette burn. They loved how she gave herself away, without a thought. Just opened up, throwing off her clothes, to some music, when there was a radio playing nearby or someone had brought one and its low light still gleamed when the sound faded because the batteries had run out. They asked for me, too. They tossed me up and caught me in the air, made me walk on my stick legs, had me touch them for luck in different places, get them up stiff where they hung limp. And I helped them wash up afterwards, splashing water or beer on them. Some came just for me, like a dress-up artist in night ladies' clothes who tried wigs on me, and a giggly fat man who bounced me around in his elastic supporter, which was like my sling. And kids sneaked in to hang basket bug wreaths on me. Once a kid who'd seen me squatting gave me a turd in a rubber sheath.

In one town they needed us at a wake. Sad people were sent to fetch us. A sort of reception committee. Bowing and backing out of our shed. A baby had died. They'd heard of Mama's baby and the angel in me. They just wanted us to be there. She wore a widow's veil: long black eyelashes that darkened her face. I was naked in my straps, because of the heat. I wasn't ashamed of being seen naked because I had my skin on. A lady who did strips had taught me that: even naked, you kept your privacy under your skin. I'd had a rash, so they powdered me all over. Mama held me up tight in my harness. We joined the mourners and weepers, in a downtown house with open doors and windows. People came in everywhere, in black veils and shawls. We sat on a cushion. Mama held her baby belly high. Some choir kids wearing paper flower wreaths put one on me. I made talky sounds. People came and petted me. Other pets gathered around me: hairless dogs with ratty tails. A breed that almost didn't exist any more, except at funerals. They couldn't bark but just sat and panted. The women counted prayer beads. They murmured and told stories. Things that were in their thoughts. We caught words here and there. Memories that made them cry. They sat in chairs that formed a circle. They lit candles and sparklers. It was more like a celebration, in spite of the tears. They burned wisps of papers with messages over the dead baby in its open box. Promises, wishes that flew up in tiny flames, on mothy wings. The baby was in a gauzy wrap like a second, transparent skin.

There was a love lady dressed in vaporous lace. She was one of those mothers who carried other people's babies. Another woman in white was a wetnurse. We knew her because she was our nextdoor neighbor in the shacks. She delivered and also drained babies in basins. She used needles and plungers. She kept their relics in lockets. Older women had washed and dressed the corpse. And flower girls, not yet love ladies, dressed as brides, sprinkled petals on it. The Marias were there. They were fiesta ladies in saints' costumes. One wore a nun's veil and breastplate, but we recognized her. They were often around, driving a pink van. I thought I saw more faces of ladies in the stains on the walls. Like the shadowy apparitions believers saw. Market women squatted fanning the heat and flies away with their skirts. There were prayers and blessings, voices droning. The mourners and weepers wailed. Streaks of black tears masked their faces. The hairless dogs panted in silence, but they stretched their necks as if they were howling. And the ashes of wishes flitted around and fell on us like dead leaves. I heard donkey braying outside. It was Papa watching over us and waiting to go. He'd managed to get back from somewhere. Mama had a loud heartbeat. But it was in her belly. People noticed and came and listened. They picked me up and kissed me. I felt myself throb and glow. My life on fire, every bone aching: that mystery in me that Mama always said I'd been born with or I wouldn't have survived. A nun came and put something crumbly between my lips. She was a Felisa. They sold communion wafers: sugary confections they made in their own bakery. And I thought I saw the dead baby let out a breath, like a specter of itself, flying off, a tiny skeleton in a flame.

We followed an All Saints road. It was a holiday season. Market crowds everywhere, fairs and spectacles. We were doing so well that we bought a second donkey, so the three of us could ride. Though soon we had to sell it to pay a fine. Another time, we played a lottery—a lady had dreamed a winning number—and lost. But Mama was carrying a new baby. I'd heard her and Papa making the baby. Singing and talking to each other in their way, out of this world. It gave Mama a new pale beauty. Frailer than other times. She looked haunted, as if it wasn't the body but the ghost of a baby she was carrying, maybe the one she'd lost before. She was afraid of losing it again along the bumpy road. At a fiesta town she stayed in our shed. A granny came in to look after her. Papa took me around to see the sights, dolled up in piñata tassels. Donkey, too, festooned with ribbons, shredded paper fringes, mirror chips, tinkly bells, trailing colored streamers and its puffs of gas and dung. Papa in a charro hat and flap trousers and spurs. We stopped at stands and shows. There was a lady saint in a glass booth who woke up from the dead, like a sleeping beauty. Different girls played the part, taking turns. I was dangling from donkey's teeth. I'd fallen off and he carried me ahead by my straps. The girls whirled me around and made me laugh so hard I wet myself. A man sold bags of soil. He said it was from a holy land. You could buy wishbones, bugs embedded in crystals, a calendar stone, a turtle shell with inscriptions, and we talked to people Papa knew from other fairs, a clown with goat horns in a devil's cape, and a jumping jack with gnomish features who told me your nose and ears and other body parts, male and female, went on growing after you were dead. Nextdoor they were playing an old record on a wind-up phonograph. The needle, a sort of fingernail, was blunted and the record ran too fast and the voices on the record sounded like birds. We looked in places where ladies dropped their clothes. All the time thinking up things and learning new moves, people showing whatever it was they could do, there was always something, and everybody knew something we didn't, Papa said. When we reached our shed, Mama was spread out on a mat having her baby. A showman with a drooping mustache wanted to charge to let us in.

We had to leave. Other towns as well, when things turned against us. Before they came for us, we'd be on the road, fading into the dust and traffic. Days and nights, we kept going, without stopping, eating whatever kids scavenged for us, sleeping on the saddle, Mama and me, and Papa on his legs, like donkey, who could wobble along in his sleep, seeing his way, as if he were wide awake.

But one day donkey left us. It had been shying at bird shadows overhead, wrenching under us till we couldn't stay on, and it took fright at a train crossing, when the barriers came down and almost trapped us, as Papa gazed up the rails, listening to a whistle, it galloped off and wouldn't answer our calls. We'd been seeing some bad sights. Men shot and dumped in ditches, heads strung from wires. Parched fields and towns with wilted markets. Truckloads of people and their animals headed out on the road. They were too fearful to pick us up. Mama couldn't walk, so Papa dragged us along in a pullcart. We'd found one toppled in a ditch and he got it out and yoked himself to it. His feet crusted and torn, he'd worn through his shoes. But he kept us on his back, almost rolling over him. Eating windblown dirt, drinking from a water bag. Mama washed his feet at night and he was up again in the morning, heaving us high when trucks bore down on us from behind. In a bright sweat all day. He attracted bees that made a buzz around him. I read road signs with Mama. Posters, billboards. I'd learned to read that way, in spite of my weak eyesight: words and numbers. We sang them out loud. I was old enough now to not just talk parrot talk, except for show. And we got into conversation with whoever went by. Stragglers in search of work, homeless families. Once we caught up with half a village laboring along the road, carrying burdens of possessions and old people on their backs. One of those groups on their way to the border and life on the other side, where they said there was work for everybody, they'd heard from relatives, at building projects, bridges, highways, factories, stockyards, world-wide fairs where Papa's inventions would be big moneymakers. Children jumped on to our cart. We pulled other people up with us. They hauled and pushed us over ruts, huddled with us in the freezing desert night, sharing their food with us, corn wraps and stringy dry meat. Bare fields around us, an empty waste, but we felt a new life in us. Mama and some men sang joy songs. Through the creaky joints of the cart we sensed the ground moving under us. One of those earthquakes Papa felt. Far away, but it hit us somehow. Long cracks had opened in the road. As if we'd willed them, out of the effort that was racking our bones. We made a stop at a ruined church with a caved-in roof, starlight shining through. The gnarled roots of dead trees raised the building off the ground on its crooked walls. Other people were already camped there. They'd lit a fire in the belltower, which was still standing, and Papa held me over it. I heard voices wondering about me. Someone said I was a little bright star fallen from heaven and that I wouldn't be around much longer. Mama saw a miracle image in a niche: a Virgin who used to be there. She'd appeared in other places, on walls and in windows. All the ladies knew about her. They said she cried real tears and had monthlies when she bled. There were pigeons up in the open dome, beating up a storm as if banging against windowpanes, trying to get out, and a cracked bell rang in the tower, and it was Papa hanging by both hands from the bell rope.

Then the Marias picked us up in their pink van with frilly curtains. We'd been running into them in weddings and wakes, where they'd be all over me, in their busty outfits and tipsy hair-dos. The minute they saw me they'd come and kiss and hug me and hang trinkets on me, hoops they slid off their arms, tinkly earrings, like birthday presents. They said they were my godmothers, that they'd always wanted a kid like me. One couldn't help crying each time she saw me. And they admired Papa, who was doing his best for us. They said he was an artist, the world was too small for him. They'd been looking for us and they swept us up in the pink van. They were headed for Bonita, a border town. Speeding up the road, playing loud music. Five of them, about all you could fit in the van, crammed in with us, blowing kisses out the windows. Free spirits with happy names: Leona, Joya, Reyna the Queen, a bossy lady, in command. And Mesias, their mighty man, a blustery type, at the wheel, which he let me hold, bouncing me on his lap. We had a joke, each time we met: he'd introduce himself, asking where we'd met before. Papa sat in front with us, after some gentlemanly maneuvering with the ladies, who made way for him, and when Mesias got off after awhile on other lady business at a bus stop, he took over the wheel. I hadn't even known he could drive, except for once when I'd seen him at the handlebar of a slow motorcycle van, running an ad. But we lurched forward, right away he had a feeling for it, and we were off, Mama holding me up between her knees, the ladies singing and carrying on. All beautied up in their glinty jewelry, one who was having dental work done even wore braces on her teeth. Another was dressed as a bride, in embroideries, with a lace veil. They had little bags of powders in secret tucks and folds, and chattered about their lives. One had almost become a nun, another had nearly married a rich man, and Queenie remembered a dramatic experience, when a man in a passion had had a fit and died in her arms. We drove all day in the heat, the ladies popping out of their props, craning out the windows to shout back at truckers who blew their horns. Their extra get-ups hung in clothes bags from hangers along a rail in back. In dust clouds they shut the windows and the van steamed up and I got carsick, and they sprayed body scents on me and tried fineries on me to entertain me, and they handed me around, pressing me against their upholstered breasts, all overheated and getting emotional, saying: "You're mine", and one who'd had to give a child away because of the life she led told me it would have been just like me.

You could sense the border, miles away. A hot river breath in the air, bleating traffic piled up on the road, wobbly carts, loaded buses tipping over on flattened tires, people hanging out the windows, trucks boiling over, stuck in potholes, the passengers getting out to push, motorcycle transports, loudspeaker vans, trailer travelers. Suddenly there were jumbles of businesses along the road: eateries, trinket shops and supply stores that sold travel equipment: coolers, money belts, backpacks, bottled water and car parts and cheap gas. Lit signs everywhere, flyers flitting around, street sales, lotteries and fun houses, trumpet bands, betting booths, job agencies, storefront churches, the whole world spilling out before us. Places where the ladies had friends who waved from doorways. At Papa, too, as if he knew them, though he wasn't saying. We barely moved, bumped along from behind into the bumper in front of us. The ladies kept jumping out a slide door to buy things. There were stretches of sidewalk, shade trees, beauty parlors. In the hazy distance we began to catch sight of a tall bridge spanning depths we couldn't see yet, and a firecrackers man came by and we got some noisemakers and threw them out the window.

We had to stop at Big Mac's, a backroom shop where we could get photo cards, which the ladies said we needed. They knew because they worked on both sides of the border, came and went in the van with their cards. We found our way up alleys, the wheels on and off curbs. People scattering out of the way, in and out of doorways. Kids selling lucky tickets, money men who sold money. Big Mac's entrance was through a dark TV Bar. The screen showed scenes from across the border: glass skyscrapers, an airport with a great wingspread, power plant towers. Distant but big as life, as if they were right outside the window. All waiting for us, said Big Mac, a sweaty man wheeling around in an armchair, in a back office. He called himself Big Mac because he'd worked on the other side, in a Big Mac restaurant, a food palace with golden arches, they were a chain and we'd seen one on this side, too. He drew us into a smoke-filled side room, flashed lights on us. He could tell we weren't just anybody. He looked at Mama in the way men did when she undressed for them, showing them how it was done. The lights went through her skin, she came out ghostly white. The ladies mugged for a picture. They needed some display photos. Big Mac took thumb prints and made us sign forms. He was some kind of an official. He had cardboard files and folders halfway up a wall. I signed with a flourish, like Papa's. The cards came out a slot in a machine: plastic face cards with our floating images. I got my own face, and on the way out we bought money from a money man, which Papa packed in a money belt.

By then it was late in the day, too late to cross. We'd heard some people didn't make it across at night. And Papa had a night job: a dig in a drainage ditch. They were building a tunnel, down under the river. He could drill and blast. Big Mac's men came for him in a truck. Its lights were out, except for a spotlight. The ladies kept the van. Some of them worked straight out of it, others in a love house, where we spent the night. It was on a busy business street. Every door and window lit up with games and ladies, palmists, dream readers with globes where things went streaming by upside down, signs with voices that said: "Become someone else. Change your name. Forget your past". Loud music out grilles, people leaning over balconies. Beauty make-over places, beds for rent in shifts, cut-you-up doctors, kids posing for pictures. A ventriloquist projected his voice to put you in touch with someone on the other side. I walked around with Mama in a soft breeze and lamplight. There were fireworks somewhere, bright as smashed glass in the sky, pinwheels whirling. I was light on my feet. Pretty as the picture on my face card, Mama said. All my bones working that night. Fiesta stardust sprinkled on us. We had our glow. We thought about where we were going. Where Papa was taking us. Mama said we'd be happy on the other side, we'd have so many more chances in life. Maybe we wouldn't be alone anymore, we'd find other people like us. We looked in joints and music bars. We came to a fun fair with peep shows. It ran all night. Gents called Mister Sams spied through slats on dancers in dazzling lights. On kids, too, baring body parts. Things they'd been growing so they could show them off. Bandera kids, some of them, doing their acts. A devil-possessed kid who was being exorcised writhed in paper flames like dragon tongues. Kids were born out of each other or hooked up in different ways. They hoarded the money people threw at them in straps and garters. I did parrot talk through a window with a kid on a chain. He jumped and bit my cheek with gums without teeth. It left a mark like a love bite. Shops hung tinsely things on me. People in balconies, too: beads and braids. Sometimes just drips of spit. And, back in the love house, Mama received visitors on her pad. They came to listen to the baby she was holding in because she wanted it to be born on the other side, nobody was supposed to know about it. Then Papa came back with burns on his arms and neck. He'd been in an explosion, but he'd caught it and thrown it off, and Mama steamed the rest of it away during the night wrapping him in wet cloths. In the morning she was still cradling him. But he was already out there in his mind, going where he meant to go.

We left at the crack of dawn. As soon as we could get all the ladies together. Reyna the Queen driving now. Papa wanted to be able to climb out and see ahead. The tide carried us along with the motor off, saving on gas, in bumps and heaves. But we hit a roadblock: flags, barriers, warning lights. A trench we had to climb in and out of. Meantime a fat Maria was having a heat stroke. So we stopped to cool off at the border cantina, leaving the van in a warehouse alley the ladies knew.

There was a bustling crowd in the dim light. Families with their bundles. People crossing on business or jobs or whatever, with day passes, factory workers, field hands. We recognized traffickers with their hand phones. We'd seen them in the villages, chatting long distance. And runners who carried things across in body holes. Some who swallowed them and pumped them out on the other side. There were all sorts of stories. Moles who burrowed through tunnels. And shifty guides who got people across in other ways. The Marias knew them all, so they moved over for us, bowing at Papa in his cape, pulling chairs out for Mama, mugging with me. We ended up at a long table, actually several tables run together. Mama got them to talk about their crossings, all along the border, we wanted to know everything. They told of times when they swam underwater, breathing through a rubber tube, or walked along the bottom of the river, through sunken junk, emptying their lungs of air, a trick they had, to weight themselves down. They floated boats or rafts, knew shallows between swampy islands in low water where you could wade across. We'd seen flippers, "frog legs", and masks with breathing tubes, on sale in shops along the road. They told of doing crazy things, even dying, to get across. People who'd drowned and been revived over there. Kids who did runs, with people or merchandise. Some almost my size, but with a swagger. There was a Rico Chico who walked around wide-legged. He was from one of the smuggling gangs, the Marias said. They had swimmer ponies and used secret paths. Other traffickers crossed on stilts. A transport service carried people across on their backs. And there was a story about a mysterious wide-backed horse called Bravo that went back and forth like a barge. We saw several big-bellied women. Some like Mama, carrying babies so they'd be born on the other side. Agents of every kind, buying and selling. Money men, a birdman with illegal birds in a bag. Felisa nuns taking orders for kids. And the hired mothers delivering babies to Mr Sams couples. Everyone dealing something, under the table or sewn into their clothes. Sick people from the other side who'd come across for a miracle medicine. You could buy a relic of someone who'd died crossing, or a picture of a Lady Liberty wearing a crown of stars and holding a torch. We drank peppery hot drinks. Boozy ladies sniffed hankies that gave out a cool breeze. I got a whiff here and there. Powders lighter than air flitted up my nose like moths. A Mesias was expressing an interest in Mama. Offering her heaven and earth, you could tell. And now Papa, instead of a whistle, pulled out a talkie thing, one of those hand phones traffickers used, it lit up with a tinkly music. He kept talking into it, gesturing as if he had a line somewhere, and listening to sounds that came in, jingles and voices.

We got going again. Packed into the van, we started and stopped every few yards. We had to help out in an accident: a spill, just ahead. One of the lopsided buses had keeled over. It had to be moved out of the way. Papa pulled people through the windows. The traffic jammed up, all the way. Buses, trailer trucks, junkers with banging doors, open-roofed cars blaring music, motor carts. A great procession escorting us. Headed for our bigger and better life. The ladies making their flap. They waved airy hankies, blew kisses, took turns sticking half their bodies out a hole in the roof. Papa walked ahead with his phone. Wired into it, with ear plugs. An antenna had shot out. He was the only person on foot in a car lane. In touch with something, like when he whistled and heard wings. Catching messages, voices. Things only he knew about.

There'd been some changes of ladies in the van. Different shades and perfumes. One got in that we hadn't seen before, dressed as a nun. She had more pockets in her folds than Papa's cape. We were a complete dress-up company. Our queen at the wheel, our nun with prayer beads, saints and a bride. And Papa leading the way. The van swung like a hammock. Mama holding herself in. She couldn't let the baby show, but it didn't look like it could wait. She grabbed me and we hung on. I was so hot that my straps stuck to me. When I raised them off my skin they left welts. The road bulged and blistered. It caved in in spots. The steaming blacktop crumbled into gravel. Cars ahead smoked us. Others rammed us from behind. Our springs screeched and gave way under us. But we got past the guard posts, with a lot of loud hellos, up a ramp, and we were on the bridge, people on either side of us shuffling along with their kids and bags, holiday shoppers, workers, the length of the wire-screened walkway. We free-wheeled, with just the push from behind to keep going. In heat waves up to our ears. A steep fall and echo beneath us. Papa still walking ahead, calling or getting calls on the phone, it even rang once. High up over the hump of the bridge. The shadowy river way below: a muddy flow with bushy banks. We'd heard of people jumping in and being fished out on the other side, beaten or shot, climbing over walls, electric fences, some thrown back in, down the embankment. Hunted with dogs, mounted police, on horses or big wheels with revolving lights, sirens. Round-ups and body searches, the ladies said. They had some fun scaring us. But at the entryway with the inspection station nothing happened. Other cars and trucks were pulled over and emptied out in a holding area, but we had friends and flashed our face cards at a glass booth and they waved us right through. Swept along on our energy, out from under the arches into the sun: a parking lot where some people dropped to their knees and kissed the hot pavement. Parked cars blazed in the lot, globes floated off high wires overhead, and pigeons from sooty factory windows flew around.

Across some rails there was a salvage yard, where the ladies dropped us off. Papa was already there looking the cars over. He had a driver's license: another Big Mac card. The ladies helped us choose and bargain. They liked lipstick colors. Mama waited in the sales shed, where there was a cool air blower. It puffed her hair into airy shapes. She was wearing our money belt. I picked my way through metal scraps and pipes. It was too hot to sit anywhere. The yard man thought I was funny. He threw cowboy hats on my head. A hearty, laughing guy, he tried different ways of talking to us, with a lot of hand language. Another man, with a loud bark, kept asking us where we were from. He'd been overbearing at first. But we weren't like other people who came in. Papa spoke in our way, with his faraway gestures. They gaped at his strange accent. And he pretended not to understand them. He listened to a sales pitch and nodded, seemed about to close a deal, then talked himself out of it. The ladies translated and explained. In the end Mama figured out what to say, and we settled on a four-door beauty, battered but still gleaming, silvery where it had scrapes, with tail fins and a flying wings hood ornament. It was all paid for, even the license plate. The ladies had contributed. They had some borrowing deal going with Mama. We sat her in front, belted up, the dashboard fan, a little whirly thing, blowing on her. We had to clear junk out of the back seat. There was also a roof rack with a torn tarp, and a slump in the floor where the springs sagged. But Papa started it right up, with a blast of the engine that sent oily smoke out the tailpipe, and got it out into the parking lot. The ladies waving loud goodbyes. Headed in another direction. As they went by, one of them reached in our window with scissors and snipped off a lock of Mama's hair. And we took off, over the train tracks and across the lot, our whirly fan going, Papa wired into his phone, the sooty pigeons spreading trash like market birds as they scattered out of our path. I was plumped in an inner tube Papa had fixed around me in the back seat, like a life preserver.

We gassed up at a station under a lit star sign, where Papa had the car raised over the pit to check its unders, while Mama and I shook bags of eaties, crispy things and chips, out of a coin machine that made change, and we guzzled fizzy drinks, and we took plastic bottles of water with us when we left, up an avenue with shopping palaces on either side, fountains, plazas, traffic lights, out on to a wide open highway. On our way, forever. That was us! Flat out into the distance. A bare tire with a blister thumped under us, a torn fender stuck out on one side like a broken wing, but we didn't care. Mama sang a chirpy song about birds flown from the nest. We even had a radio that broke out every now and then in twangy sounds. Hot wind blasted in the windows and vents like brassy music. Our rooftop tarp flapped like a sail. Road signs ahead pointed to places hundreds of miles away, in every direction. We had sightings: overpasses connecting loops of roads on high, a flashing airport beacon. Things we'd seen on Big Mac's TV screen, suddenly right there. Papa tuned into it all with his phone. He said he'd bought time. He let us listen: it picked up chitchat, tire noise, sirens, a hollow ring, like some sort of space music that had faded before it reached us, or maybe just the buzz of high wires. The dashboard needles flipped back and forth, so we didn't know our speed. But we were flying with our hopes, above and beyond ourselves, as Papa said we had to be, stretching out toward the distant haze that let through floating images of towns, metal towers. We drove along fields sunk in oily waves, like a hot ocean, with horsehead-shaped pumps working, fires flaring and breaking up into their reflections, as if in an air made of melting mirrors. Our horn stuck, honking on its own, the motor coughing but running in gusts, after we'd had to pull out on to the shoulder and Papa had tinkered under the hood with tools he'd found in the trunk, and then he'd jacked us up to change the bad tire for a retread, with fast-going traffic blowing us back and forth, and the whole time he was placing and receiving calls on the phone, which he'd connected to the battery, by somehow plugging it into the radio, through the lighter, so it would charge while we were on the road, and firing up to full speed he got us into a maze of ramps winding up into an overlook from where we saw a sun-bleached airport, with its runways, decks, glassed-in walks, a lighthouse watchtower with a starburst sign crowning it, planes landing and taking off like monster birds, and he threw his arms out the window and said it was all ours.

We spent the night in a night park: a car rest off the road with sleeping lanes. A place to power up, next to some heaving trucks with night lights parked side-by-side, pulsing with energy, the motors running. The service building throbbed. Landscaped and lit up, it made my head ache. We swung through a double door. They had wall maps, vending machines, toilets that flushed themselves. We tried everything out, washed up with oozy soap at taps that turned themselves on and off. There were dry air spouts instead of towels. Mama changed me, since I'd had an accident and we found a paper diaper dispenser in a wall slot, and we packed some extra diapers for the road. We filled out water bottles at an icy cold drinking fountain. Papa, in his haste, knocked over a trash bin on his way out, with a rolling noise, down the walk. We'd found a shady spot, at the far end. Past cars with families locked inside, a pet area where loners walked watch dogs. A path led into some trees, where pick-up ladies waited at a picnic table. Big blondes, and a dark lady with a blonde wig, and their Mesias manager. We saw him hovering nearby. We wrapped ourselves up inside our car. In a feverish huddle, thinking of the next day. Things and places we imagined. Endless farmlands, great cities. We'd left the ceiling light on by mistake and people came by and looked in at us. A police car roved with a spotlight. A motorcycle gang stopped off in capes and flying skull-and-bones flags. Truckers rocked the car to make fun of us. It went on half the night. I woke up several times in my inner tube. Papa was walking back and forth outside, taking calls. Mama was short of breath, she had to get out. She was gone for a long while. Up the path into the trees. I couldn't get my stiff bones going to follow her. But she came back looking much better. She had her night bloom, like a moonflower. She'd loosened her clothes, she wore nothing under her slip dress. She let Papa make her comfortable. Fitting his body into hers, making her sigh. It happened when they had their moments of happiness together. And they included me, gathered in Mama's arms, she rocked and sang me to sleep with a song about a bird that flew down to nest in my eyelashes.

We set out at daybreak. Into our bright new morning. A sweep of clear sky. People and their businesses were already up and going. All-night places along the road still blazing. Trucks sucking up energy at a gas station, the Lone Star sign in a neon halo up high, when we pulled in, and some men hanging around the pump, acting friendly, made Papa drink from the hose with them.

Back on the road an armed patrol riding big tires flagged us down, but I did my parrot talk, by then I knew how to sound like them, and they let us go, before Papa got worked up. We stopped at a dollar store, a sort of indoor fair we'd noticed in several places, with half its goods, yard stuff, housewares, spilled out the entrance. First chance we had, we'd been wanting to stock up on water, beauty products for Mama, and check out the toys and gadgets Papa liked to handle, somehow getting his fingers into the packages, which were all sealed. There were soap suds in the air, candy smells, bug sprays, scented paper flowers. Women in dollar store dresses, which were like underwear, were loading up on bags of goodies and Papa wheeled me around in a shopping cart, as if I couldn't walk. Up and down the aisles, just for the pleasure of being in such a world of fluffy toilet paper and body-size bottles. We bought a contraption for me, a walker we found discarded in a torn box, with legs on tiny wheels and a chin-high bar like a balcony rail. On sale and ready to use if I ever needed it, it could almost walk on its own. All eyes in the shop watched me as I tried it out, creaking and twisting to get into a ring that fitted around my waist, and a girl at the cash register stuck a sunny face sticker on me as I hobbled out in it, and it folded into itself and I clung to it in the back seat of the car, the pop-out wheels replaced with cork plugs by Papa so I could lean on steady legs when I got off.

We drove all day, seeing the sights. Hazy flatlands, oil-fields with their burn-off fires. Papa knew what everything was. We saw things even before they were there. Billboard signs flared up with images: a night-lit ballpark, a skyscraper city. They weren't just ads: it was all somewhere. Life and space opening up in us. A smoldering patch of land we passed was a lake bottom, Papa said. It had houses floating in heat waves. In the middle of nowhere, we stopped to climb a ladder up a watchtower to a terrace with a telescope on a stem like a parking meter. Papa shook it to loosen some coins inside and we pointed it all around, getting the lay of the land. Even without it, things out of sight came into view. I was in the top spot, on Papa's back. We saw birds soaring over a dust bowl: a place called Vista Valley. Somewhere else, a giant outdoor movie screen stuck out over a highway with clouds or shadows, it was hard to tell what they were in the daylight, running across the surface, like the shapes on the face of the moon. All this Papa gave us.

He was already gone that night. On some job he'd picked up. We'd stopped at a diner. Not one of the fancy lit places. A smoking clapboard shed off the road. We had to go over a trench to reach it. Past an oil town, in an encampment with drill towers, construction trailers and a bunkhouse. We braked nose first at the door. Sniffed the air and ordered, off a menu board, all their strange eats: fried steaks, some kind of jerked meat, bacon drippings, sausages. We'd saved for that moment. A bucket of grits, a gallon of soda. And it didn't matter if we couldn't pay for it all. They needed an extra hand at some machinery out in the fields. A man had tested Papa's grip in a handshake. And Mama didn't mind working wherever she was appreciated. There was a facility across from the diner: a trailer with a blinking sign showing a bare-breasted beauty. A black Mac ran the place: ladies in boots and shorts. They talked hard talk but loved Mama with her happy-hearted laugh. They kept me in the bunkhouse so I couldn't get away. A tobacco-chewing lady watched over me. We drank something that made me woozy. She kept bending to catch me when I lost my balance. When I woke up in a bunk, and Mama hadn't come back yet, the night was bright with fires. We went out where there was a portable jail cell with a toilet. Sort of like a roadside chapel, with a man tied up inside. You could just make him out in the dark. She wanted him to say something and he tried to talk to me, but I acted deaf and dumb. Papa had said there was a law protecting kids like me, no one could touch me. But I was worried about him. There'd been armed men in his work crew. And the black Mac wouldn't let Mama go, they'd been shouting and arguing. But they both broke away somehow and they came honking for me, halfway through the night, while everyone was partying in the firelight. Papa even had his wages, and Mama was hiding extra money in the upholstery. And he was on the phone, taking a call.

We kept moving, for several days. With only short stops at rest stops. A couple of hours, till we attracted attention, and we were gone. Looking ahead, whatever happened. Fast as light on our thumping tires. Eating out of our dollar store reserves, and grits and beans once a day, at a chili house. We tried a fry house, a pancake house, even a Big Mac once with its golden arches. In and out of Lone Star stations for gas. Another dollar store for supplies. Our money going out the window. Riding the airstream and truck tailwinds. Until it got dark, suddenly, we hardly noticed the light fading, only that we were straining to see. Our headlights aimed everywhichway, Papa hadn't had a chance to work on them. So, one night, we pulled up for the night in a shopping center parking lot attached to a big box store with a spread of dependencies, storage and unloading areas, potted trees along the edges of the lot, lit by a vapor of arc lamps. A noisy night life had gathered there: trucks with glowing underbellies, rolling houses, campers opened up with all their equipment: pop-up tops,

sliding doors, fold-out porches and steps, shower
stalls, bug screens, charcoal grills, music players, so
we settled right in, strung a hammock for me from
two lamp posts, and while Papa unloaded trucks all
night long in back of the big box, after we'd had our
beauty rest I went visiting with Mama, like in our
market days. Airing out in our skimpy dresses. She'd
cut mine from a larger size, with plenty of breathing
space, so it kept me cool when I was feverish, in
spite of my bindings. And they asked us in places.
Happy people, vacationers, with decks and sitting
rooms, traveling in their homes on wheels with their
built-in furniture. They invited us around, sat us on
pull out beds, a cushion or bean bag for me, drinking
iced tea, vents blowing on us. They tried to talk to us,
looking expectantly at Mama, as if she were giving
out advice when she nodded and smiled. They took
instant pictures of us, and while Mama stayed on and
carried on her conversation I made some friends,
kids on skateboards, wheeling by, they grabbed
hold of me and pushed and pulled me along in my
walker, to see how far I'd go. I couldn't keep up, but
I could talk like them, once I got going, and make
them laugh. They poked me all over, wondering how
I worked. One had a flying toy he controlled with
a buzzer, and he pretended he could buzz me, too.
And a little girl had a doll that spoke to me, deep
in its throat, where there was a voice on a tape. Its
arms and legs came off on springs and it hung its
head. It reminded me of when I bounced in my sling.
It was too much excitement for me and I had some
kind of a breakdown, lost my grip, and sprawled on
the pavement. My eyes blurred. I felt all my bones

come loose, as in my worse days. Even my teeth and hair seemed to be falling out. With my parrot talk I couldn't explain myself. People were impressed by the straps and buckles that stuck out under my skirt. I was even wearing a pretty girdle. Men from an ambulance came with an air tank, they wanted to put a breathing mask on me, but Mama wouldn't let them. Instead, she got into our hammock with me and we swung in the night air. In the morning Papa was lying under the car, fixing a loose pipe or a leak.

The next days we drove around, taking things in. Papa on the phone, picking up messages, job prospects. Radio voices kept bursting in, ads and announcements. Sometimes cowboy music, or just sound waves. It all meant something. High-pitched signals like bird cries. We stopped wherever there was work. Papa talking his way in, walking out if he didn't like the offer. He didn't sell himself cheap. And he had his resources. A Mister Sams in a warehouse employment office would know of a factory that was hiring packers, a basement workshop that needed a watchman. We'd like the look of a place, some bright little town without sidewalks where everybody drove to get anywhere, trucks and farm kids riding tractors, and there'd be a a night house in an alley where a lady friend got Mama a late shift and Papa a door job, while I slept in the car. Vagrants out of bars at dawn would try to get in. One of them had a walker like mine, only without the ring. And we'd got a business going in towns with street sales. Dollar store gimmicks we resold. Lip whistles, glow toys, touched up by Papa so people didn't recognize where they came from, sticky hands and jumping spiders we pulled out of goody bags, on rubber bands. I had a funny-face bug I'd stolen, to make it more mine. A wriggly worm that grew wings when you squeezed it. Everyone thought it was real when I dangled it out the window. Another time we did a job for a church. We'd parked overnight in the church lot. The neon cross threw an eerie light on us. It clung to Mama's skin and hair, which had silvery white strands. People inside the church heard our radio playing their music, a broadcast that reached us from across the border, and they took us in. Because they were migrants like us, only without border cards. They were hiding and traveling whenever they could catch a ride. They'd left families behind, they showed us pictures, talking in a rough-made language of whispers they'd developed, so they could stay in touch over distances in the dark, and in the morning we dropped some of them down a side road, and they asked Mama for her blessing.

Soon we were in cattle country, endless miles of it. Wild grasses where horned beasts grazed, feed lots, weather ponds, stockyards, and a different sky above, with storm clouds, split by flashes of lightning. A dark sun smoldering behind it all. And every few miles an air strip. Jets streaking off into space. Once, silent wings glided right above us, trailing a streamer of words. Then a duster plane buzzed us going by. More oil fields blazed ahead. There was always something going on. Everything brought us images. Windmill farms, sun flares, a hot-air balloon festival. Papa gathering energy and inspiration. In some stretches Mama had to steer for him when he flew off in his thoughts. We sailed through neon-lit strips with food palaces, Lone Star gas stations, drive-in hotels. Big Mac arches everywhere. A great power span. We did sightseeing runs, following a house on wheels, a billboard truck with posters showing mountains, lakes, beaches, every place you might want to go, a Holy Land Park, a Meteor Crater, a tower from where a rocket was blasting off. In a rest area TV screen we saw a desert of colored rocks, caverns with waterfalls, an echo canyon. We could have gone on forever, except when we stopped for one of Papa's big-shoulder jobs. He drove a fork lift in a hay harvest. Mama dressed me up in funny clothes in a scarecrow factory. He helped raise scaffolding for a wheel at a fair and bought us rides. At a busy crossroads there was a livestock show. A big production place, they called it the cow palace. Papa was good with the animals: they listened to his whistles. I could talk to them, too, and they'd follow me. At night I felt their warm damp breaths. At moments I was like one of them. Someone would come up and pet me. There was music and some stomping and dancing. Papa played the harmonica. He'd picked up the skill in minutes from one of the cowhands. Some kids did lasso tricks. I showed them how I twisted in and out of my straps. I hadn't been needing my walker. Mama had learned yodeling, their form of cracked voice singing. We smoked a corn-cob pipe. A cool smoke that calmed my pains. We slept in a hayloft. It was quiet after the last cow lowed. We didn't mind the sting bugs or smelling of dung. Until we had to leave one morning. The flapping of pigeons woke us up, instead of the usual twitter of birds. Ready to go because they were after us, Mama said. There'd been a round-up at the dance hall down the road, where she'd been making acquaintances. So we were off again. For days, without work. Only some quick sidewalk sales. Though with Papa's skills we could have stayed almost anywhere. But we wanted something more. And we might be found out at any time, Mama said, I might be taken away. There was some kind of child police. They'd want me to go to school, or I'd end up in a home. So we drove around endlessly. Papa with his sightings. Or just riding along. Wherever the road took us, we couldn't go wrong. Once we passed a stadium with a sky dome. A noisy ball game was on, a great spectacle we could almost see, when it broke out over our radio. And Papa was on the phone every minute, we could tell, wired in somehow even when he wasn't using it, the calls still came in. Saving on expenses, we stopped to eat in places where they didn't charge us for the meal when they saw me in my walker, and at truck stops to load the phone, which could be plugged into an outlet, and Papa would rent a locker and leave some money in it, in case of an emergency, if we came that way again.

We spent a few nights in one of those drive-in hotels. The sign drew us in: a thunderbird, with blazing wings. Cars with license plates from different places were already wedged side by side into parking slots. We paid for a night in advance, with a fifty dollar bill. We didn't have to say who we were. Mama, who needed her privacy, got a separate room. We waited up for her, doing some exercises Papa had invented for me, which were really mind exercises, because I could do them even when I couldn't move, and in the morning we drove around, while maids made our rooms, then Mama got some sleep and afterwards she gave herself a bubble bath, while she washed our clothes, and I helped her pretty up, picking colors from her beauty kit, and she punched up a fat cushion for me before going. And we waited again. Worried because we didn't know who'd be calling on her, Papa couldn't sleep, even stretched out full length on the double bed with a luxury mattress. But she rang us a couple of times over the room phone. She was laughing and enjoying herself. And we were all right from then on. We'd figured out how much we owed the hotel office. They were hot bright nights. Made for us, Papa said. He kept me up all night. We had a drinking fountain and coin machine supplies in a gallery, down a metal staircase. Talk and TV chatter seeped through the walls from the neighboring rooms. Cars came and went, parked right outside our window. I watched them through the curtains. Latecomers who didn't stay long. I could tell time from the nighttable clock. It ticked when the minute hand jumped. Papa would be working on some idea. He got restless and took me out with him. We'd walk along the edge of the strip in traffic. The sky reflected the lights back on us. I didn't use my walker. He said I'd make it. There was a bar with a jukebox nearby. He liked the music, which seemed to play itself. He'd pick out some notes and hum them. He could do that with any music, as if he'd heard it before. But he was listening to something else. Men sat on high stools motioning and seeing things. A man shaped figures with his hands. Another dangled his fingers like puppets on strings. They let me in with Papa so they could have a look at me. They admired my walk. They said I was going places. They sat me on the bar and made me talk. The bar girl wanted to hold me. She kept asking me where I was going. They joked with Papa, too, wondering how far he could fly in his cape. He played jukebox tunes for them on beer can tabs. Sometimes he had to carry me back to the hotel. Once we were just in time for him to do one of his great jobs. There was a fire in the next room, the smoke came through the walls, and he rushed straight in, knocking down the connecting door, and brought a baby out rolled in his sleeves. After that they let us stay for a week for free. A good thing because I was having the shakes. But we hid it so they wouldn't throw us out. I kept moving when the maid came in to vacuum. Back and forth between Mama's room and Papa's. Kids waited on the walk and sprayed me with fire extinguisher foam. Then, when we were about to leave, they needed another cleaning woman and they hired Mama, and we stayed on. They didn't know who we were. It hadn't been revealed yet, Papa said. He'd been talking that way. I had a feather duster to catch spiderwebs. Mama pushed towels and sheets on a dolly, wearing a smock. One of our many disguises till our time came, Papa said.

At another place, a shopping mall, called Star City—we'd stopped because they were giving kids shots out of a health van in the parking lot and one might be good for me— birds flew around. Some got trapped in ceiling panels. Papa reached out and set them free. I helped him, riding on his back. We did odd jobs, at stores that were being torn down or set up. We slept in an empty shop, on a sort of air bed that covered the floor. Mama made it cozy. There was a food court and a sprinkling fountain. Our reflections met us in show windows we'd washed. It seemed like Papa's magic. He'd gesture as if raising us out of ourselves. He could do it at any time. He wheeled me around in a wheelchair you could borrow, a rolling throne. Only fat people and cripples used them. His long stride swept me along. We left Mama in a beauty shop. They were doing hair-styling demonstrations. It was also a love lady business. They had an attic and a basement. At a cowboy store I tried on a longhorn hat and boots with studs. They were surprised when I got out of the wheelchair without help. I was wearing an elastic back brace Papa had invented. On my good days I could even run a few steps. I practiced letting go of my walker. By now it was just the handrail, without the inside ring, which I'd outgrown. Papa let me ride the escalator. As we took a step up he said we were going faster than the belt carrying us along. And, afterhours, in another lightning change, we slipped into work clothes and joined a clean-up crew with scrub brushes and trash bins on casters. I got my bones moving, and some rags, and I mopped on hands and knees, and Mama spread freshening air from a can.

We did some long car days. Papa could sleep at the wheel and still see ahead. He woke up when we ran out of gas. Coasting along, on to the shoulder or into a ditch. And a car always stopped to help, as if Papa had called it in. They had every kind of equipment. Even on an out-of-the-way road, someone rolling by in a pick-up, helloing with his wide-brim hat, would run a hose from his gas tank into ours, or jump-start us, when Papa's home-made battery charger didn't work, and hang around till we got going. Once a road assistance van reached us. We'd been backfiring and blowing black smoke. They had a number you could call. I was feeling ill in the heat and throwing up. I'd had a crazy spell with nightmares and started kicking and pulling out my hair, I couldn't help myself. They wanted to take me somewhere. But by then I'd pulled myself together. And we were already going somewhere, Papa said. He kept reminding me, and Mama too: I'd find my way. Our headlights were dim that night, Papa kept them low, we drove almost in the dark, but we saw the tower of a truck stop sticking out through some trees, a Lady Liberty with her crown of stars and spikes, holding a torch high in one hand. We'd been there before: an all-night city. It was one of the places where we'd left money in a locker. There were stores and jobs. An all-weather tire sellout, a body shop with a pit. And lit corridors inside, game rooms, toilets, coin machines with snacks, a TV map room, even sleeping rooms with bunks. Papa got work in the car wash, where they were short a hand. They paid by the hour, so it was like being self-employed. He made a great splash hosing down the trucks, in a slop suit. And it turned out Mama knew the hostess in the bar. They went off together. She had her bloom and people noticed her. There were other beauties in lounge chairs, with gorgeous hair-dos, slit skirts and necklines, but she stood out. I waited for her at a corner table under a lamp where a lady wearing colored glasses was doing accounts. They gave me a mug with a face to drink out of. Another kid who sat next to me spiked my drink out of a pocket flask. He wouldn't take his hot eyes off me. It was almost like a love look. The lady let me see through her glasses and everything seemed bigger and clearer. People with loud voices, faces in bottles. The soft bar light was on my skin. I felt flushed and glittery. Then Mama took me around the shops. She'd found our locker with the money, and she'd made some more. There was a convenience store that sold all sorts of supplies: batteries, tobacco, coolers, bandages, and personal stuff, ladies' things, toiletries, sunglasses, tampons, diapers. The cashier gave me a teddy bear to hold while we were in the store and took it back when we left. A gift shop sold pretty cards, trinkets, hair bands and bows, scented candles, anything you could think of. We tried things on and felt glamorous. Shoppers said we looked alike. We bought make-up and went out blowing on a pinwheel with daisy petals. It made a trill, like a bird, and brought Mama a memory, and she began to cry, without a sound, quiet tears, with just a whisper in her breath, like when she sang to me. It happened when she was thinking of that other life she longed for with people like us. Ghostly people she barely remembered, maybe they'd never even met, but close as family, waiting for us somewhere where we'd be ourselves. Anything could bring it on. I imagined them as bony people, like me, but in a former life, Papa's other world. The only picture I had of it was the messenger pigeons, which Papa had told me once he used to own, when he had a pigeon house. And Mama had once shown me a tiny bright stone she hid in different parts of her body, a family jewel she called it, which she'd had to sell. It was all in the spin of the daisy wheel. We went and sat in the car, with the motor on for company, people leaning in the windows to make comments, till Papa got back. And driving out, from an overpass, we saw a wreck on the highway below, smoke and fire, the traffic a mighty sea, backed up for miles, and a helicopter whirling overhead, shining a spotlight down, and Papa held me up above the guard rail to watch.

And one day it just happened. In a town with a lurid light. Rips of lightning in the dark sky. A dry storm had blown by. Papa had walked off some job in another town. They'd been pushing him out. One of those times he was too big for them. People not worth half of him but organized. They'd tried to take away his card. We'd raged out on to the highway and wandered on an almost empty gas tank. Freewheeling when we picked up enough speed to cut off the motor and keep going, Papa knew exactly how to do it. We still had our radio, and we could get calls on the phone. Delivery trucks bumpered us from behind going into this new town, over a railway crossing with a clanging bell. There were pigeons flapping off the ledges of buildings, cornices and windowsills. Papa saw his chance: on an impulse, we veered and drew into a free parking lot on the approach to downtown and got out and walked. Mama wasn't well and stayed in the car. We left her in the shade under a warehouse roof. A town bus had stopped in the lot with a flat, waiting for rescue. They had air-conditiioning and asked her in. Nice people who wanted to help. They thought she might be pregnant. You could tell by the way they handled her. Meantime we headed dowtown. Papa with his

loping gait, I shambled along. I couldn't keep up, so
he hoisted me on his back. We stood way out over
even the tallest bighats. A jostling crowd had come
out after the storm. Shoppers, office workers loitering
in doorways. A Salvation Army band blew horns
and banged on a collection kettle. It must have been
some special time of the year. The stores were all lit
up in the daytime. Clothing stores, coffee shops, an
indoor market, a gun shop, worlds of things, a wax
museum with figures that looked like real people,
a mirror house and other shows and amusements,
scarecrow displays with clown clothes, a horsehead
jack pumping in a show window, a meeting hall
of some kind where people walked in, straight off
the street, and sang in a choir, on benches rising
like a staircase into the open roof, where sunlight
broke in. We made our way toward a clock tower.
Papa with his phone out, and a lot of pigeons in the
trees. Messy birds flying about like ashes over the
town square, sprinkling their droppings, gathering
in from the parking lots and down from the clock
tower and rooftops and eaves, bringing messages.
And suddenly Papa stepped off the curb, I felt the
jolt, and he was doing his pigeon sweep, he waved
the birds to the ground and back up again and away,
in a storm of feathers, like burned papers going up a
chimney. A tremendous gesture, it stopped the traffic,
people gaped in awe. I was also up there waving.
And, before anyone could interfere, we moved on to
the next block, where he did it again, carried away,
deeper and higher, still bearing me on his shoulders,
hustled along by a growing crowd and the cops that
had been following us. Feathers rained down on us,

and I caught money bills, and the way Papa swept some pigeons into his cape and back out his sleeves, I realised he wasn't just receiving messages but sending them.

As we reached the other end of town, our car came up behind us, Mama at the wheel, we saw her smile. All for show, just steering, since she couldn't drive, but following us, pushed along by some kids in a pick-up, through a red light. And she slid over for Papa, while I piled in behind, and he got us started, with roaring thunder, and we were off again, along car lots and a scrap metal dump, then out on the strip, where we loaded up at a gas station with flying windsocks, and on past golden arches and a thunderbird motel, and afterwards more wide open cattle country, endless feed lots, into the next town, in time for the electric night, which lit up with flaring neon signs, jigsaw figures of ads and shooting stars, and on through town, and on the other side, miles out, where the road got shadowy, there was a huge drive-in movie screen, just off the road, where we spent the rest of our money to park and watch flickering images of people and places that seemed to be inside our eyes, like figures in a dream.

The next days we did several shows. There were always pigeons in a parking lot or the town square. Other performers did their numbers: talkers, picketers, cowboy singers, but we were different in our way of being, in and out of our own world, like the messenger pigeons, coming and going. In some towns they already knew about us. Cars tooted at us, people yodeled and waved. A drunk would ask for a lift. He'd yank at the doors as if to rip them off.

We'd get out at a red curb or a hydrant. We had a few minutes to call in the pigeons. They'd come beating down on us, raising paper trash off the sidewalk, and I'd pick out the money bills, catching them in the air, street kids scrambling after the ones I missed. Sometimes we didn't even have to stop, the pigeons flew in and out the windows. We'd be moving along, a ten-ton truck ramming us from behind. Loud music everywhere, greeting us. People with sound boxes, amplifiers. Horns blowing when we stalled. Even when we ended up in jail we got special treatment. A respectful officer seated Mama on a wide padded seat while Papa signed a book. They emptied his pockets and couldn't believe all the things they found, and listed them. They let Mama keep her money belt. She was making her baby. They'd noticed it in a strip search. Sometimes just from her milky white complexion. We posed for photos, and she was radiant. They treated me like some breakable doll. They tried to get me to speak. I'd make them laugh with my antics. Others stared or looked away. They settled us all together in a cool cell, Papa wouldn't allow us to be separated, and when we were, it was only overnight. We left him in the light, they never put it out. In some prisons they were on a death watch, Mama told me. She'd heard it from her lady friends. People were killed overnight, or they killed themselves. When we couldn't stay with Papa, a matron would take care of us, in a women's house. She'd be a nurse or a policewoman, rough but friendly. She understood our broken language, even spoke a few words. She'd ask Mama about me, listen to my parroty talk. She'd show us pictures of her family: men and women in cheery colors, with bright hair-dos, kids my age. She helped Mama give me a bubble bath. People came in to look. And we were happy all night, in clean white bedsheets. I'd lie there loosened up without any bindings, my welts and sores healing. In the morning we got Papa out. They'd given him back most of his things. Sometimes they'd let him go earlier, Mama said he'd escaped. He'd find us, wherever we were, having rescued the car from the tow yard, and we'd be out on the road again.

Out in the open range, whistling in the wind. Bulldog-noses trucks running us down or splattering gravel back at us. Showers of bugs bursting on the windshield. Papa with some kind of road map in his head. Lit up like one of those maps in glass panels at Lone Star stations. Awake or asleep in the glare, we kept going. With quick stops at fast food palaces, where you ate on trays. They'd see me struggling and let us ahead in the line. Sometimes we ran out of money. We'd been counting on our savings in a locker, but we'd lost the key. So we did some sweat work for a meal. We didn't accept charity. Whatever happened, we remembered who we were. In a town where people shook our car and nearly pulled us out—we'd been there before with our show, but they'd turned against us—a two-car police patrol escorted us out of town.

In the next town, where there was a carnival, Papa found work for a week setting up games and rides. He had to beat the pigeons off. There was a water slide, which was good for me, and he bounced me in a bounce house. They kept him up late into the night, when gangs roamed, in loud cars, starting trouble. I stayed with Mama in a safe house run by some ladies. They were women who helped other women who hid there, for various reasons, made comfortable, in homey furnishings, with bedsteads, body-hugging armchairs, battered chests of drawers. They had bruises and broken bones, and they told Mama their stories, and she talked to them, and most of the time they didn't know what she was saying but they liked the sound of her voice, and they all wanted to listen to her baby.

Wherever we stayed, women would come and take her into their rooms or a back porch, seesawing on a swing chair, wherever she was needed, they said she gave them life. In one of the houses there was a lady who made clothes, all sorts of fancy designs, love lady dresses. She put fashion touches on Mama, silky stockings, a gauze scarf. She'd seen me naked, in a hot bath. She said I had a pretty blush. Another woman made me laugh when I was aching. She called herself Ladybird. She walked me on tiptoes, like a dancer, and promised she'd adopt me if Mama was sent back or I was taken away. They all mothered and spoiled me. They taught me things, like how to look at myself in the mirror from the best angle. They had me bending in every direction. I could reach almost anywhere. Some houses had a schoolroom, to keep the kids off the streets, so they wouldn't be kidnaped or beaten up. In one place they gave me a birthday party with a cake and balloons. We burst a bag of party favors. Some of them were Papa's inventions: toy whistles, paper birds, flower buds that opened in water. A woman said she'd lost a kid like me. We made a wish together. She was one of the ladies in hiding. She wore dark glasses, so I never saw her eyes, only my reflections. I looked like Mama, wise and beautiful. When the women were busy with each other they put me out back with their kids, who were afraid of me, they'd never seen anyone like me. And I had this feverish desire to play with them, I didn't care what we did, I'd run up and hug and kiss them. They'd take me to see something in an alley and leave me. Itching with excitement, the next moment I'd turn my head and they'd be gone.

One time I was in such pain, and almost not noticing it, accustomed to being myself, that the ladies made arrangements. A hospital came for me. They wanted to look me over. I was so strange they took x-rays. They said I was messed up inside. Tied up in knots. They tapped on my bones. They pricked me all over to get samples. I thought they were going to take me apart. I'd heard, from the kids, that they cut you up and used your pieces for someone else. They wheeled me around on a stretcher. I was bound, hands and feet. They shined a light in my eyes. For a while I couldn't see. They left me in the dark, wired into a machine that ticked and purred. Mama held my hand. A playful doctor asked me if I'd fallen off a wall. He said they were going to put me back together. I thought of those dolls made of a skull and bones with real hair and teeth. They tried to get me to wear a metal brace. It clamped shut and trapped you inside. But I didn't need anything, Mama said, I was fine just the way I was, I had a mystery, something nobody else had. We got away, and after that we slept in the car, in a pay lot, which was safer when other cars blinked their lights at Mama. I was still wearing the hospital wrist strap. I locked myself in with the motor and the dashboard fan on while she was gone. When someone banged on the window I crawled through a hole in the back seat to hide in the trunk.

Meantime Papa was off on some big job: an oilfield or highway project. Cars and trucks would come for him. Big Macs and Mister Sams and their crews. He'd be gone for days, in demand everywhere, he could have had a contract if he'd wanted one, doing the work of several men, they wouldn't let him go. He'd make his way back on his own, hitching rides, till it became too dangerous, we'd heard armed bands picked people up and dropped them across the border. So he began taking the car with him, leaving us along the way in some roadhouse with cots for rent or a cabin motel by a creek where I could sleep in a screened porch, if there were bugs, with the breeze of running water and neighbors watching over me while Mama was out.

Another night, we settled in a lighted lot, downtown. Blazing lamps on all night. We'd washed and polished the car. It wasn't some piece of junk. It looked bright and elegant. And we'd had the windows tinted in a body shop. We could look out without being seen. There was a construction site over the lot. Half a block of pounding work. A great earth-splitting hulk rising from underground. They parked their equipment in the lot: machinery, coils of wiring, drills, a cement mixer, toilet sheds. They worked overnight. Papa had a late shift, on an open elevator. He'd kept us with him. We saw him going up and down the face of the building along a rack, in a belt, like a mountain climber. We'd had some trouble earlier, people pushing us around or trying to get hold of me, but nobody bothered us in the lot, even with the windows down. The noise and the glare kept us awake, and we sat and watched, and things got even more spectacular. A hot wind blew and there was an electric storm, in the middle of the night. Bone-breaking thunder, lightning that slashed down like zippers in the sky. The lamplight went off and came back on, powered by a heart-pounding generator. By then most of the men were gone. The rest took refuge under tarps that beat about. Some tried to get in with us. A metal roof, a big sheet of noise, tore loose and flew off in the wind. A crane swung its neck up high. We didn't know where Papa was. We thought we'd seen him sliding down a fire engine ladder. We huddled in the car and waited. The town all around us was dark. The parking lot lamps were out, too. There was only our bit of light, inside our tinted windows. When the storm died out, street sweeping machines came by, like night animals, with beeps and flashes. In the morning a plow truck piled up rubble. Papa was at the wheel, in storm clothes. There were dead pigeons in the lot, and he jumped off ahead of the shovel and threw some back into the air.

We found ways and places. There were pigeons everywhere, in barns and belltowers, dropping down on us from overpasses along the highway, or winging around like crows or vultures in the fields, shadows dumped out of the air, perched clawing on the branches of scrawny trees that withered under their weight in factory back lots. Long-distance birds way out in the sky, garbage birds in alleys. I heard their commotion in my sleep, in the back of the car, woke up as if swallowing feathers. Once I thought Mama was a pigeon. She was holding me, cooing and gurgling. Like when I was a baby and ate out of her mouth. I'd been crumpled up in the trunk. A sure place for pigeons was a graveyard. We'd spot a patch of dead pasture up a lane, behind some gnarled bushes or in back of some scattered houses or a trailer park that made a small living space in the open range, and there'd be headstones and pigeons landing on them. Sooty city birds that seemed to have flown up chimney flues. Sometimes wild doves that hunters shot at. We'd stop on an approach and Papa would make some calls. Through his teeth when he didn't want his whistles to be seen. We'd watch people laying wreaths. There were fancy carved crosses. Others were just ragged stakes, like scarecrow skeletons. The pigeons stirred up a wind, scattering leaves and flowers. Once we came on a burial, with luxury cars and mourners. Heartbroken women, sweaty men melting through their clothes. A wailing music came from a speaker on a pole. Painted eyes ran down faces in colored tears. A preacher spoke in a rich voice, deep as an echo in a well. The diggers dug out the hole and lowered the widow into it, after the box. She wanted to be down there for awhile. We stood on a patch of lawn, at a short distance, accompanying them. They hadn't seen us at first. But then they let us stay on as mourners. Papa had an elegance in his cape, a weatherbeaten force. As if he'd mastered life and death. And they liked having me around in my walker, I could tell, it made them feel better about their loss. Mama, wearing a mantilla, said a prayer, in our words. They let her through and she got the widow to come out of the hole, into her arms. And Papa waved the pigeons off.

There were pigeons in churches. Lots of them, in every town, which had several churches, with their burial plots and spires. Quiet churches with a bare altar or bright as a jukebox, with singing voices, whatever the atmosphere, any one of them might have pigeons in the rafters or flying out of the organ. We'd go in and look and listen. Heads turning toward us. Sometimes people who spoke in a strange tongue, one they prayed in. Or they'd stand up and talk out loud. And we'd slip up the aisle. With just elbow space around us. Once Papa went all the way. He sat at the organ, leaned on it and played. It made a huge music and light that shook the building, sending out dazzling shadows. Majestic, the organ was called. Its name was on a bronze plaque. You just had to touch it to get it started. It had a carved picture of a heavenly choir. Certain chords set off ringing bells. I hadn't known Papa could play. Like the time he'd taken over from the music man at a fair, and so many other unexpected things he could do, when he remembered them. He'd stepped out of our pew, muffled in his cape, and put his weight on the keyboard. It was easy, once it got started, it did most of the work on its own. We'd dressed for the occasion. We'd slept in a camper park with tap water so we could wash up, and stopped at a coin laundry to do our clothes, while we waited, wrapped in sheets we found in a dryer, and at a beauty shop for Mama, who wanted to look her best. The organ pumped itself up, Papa stepped on the pedals, pulled valves and stops, plugs and buttons, and the sound soared, as if it were Papa himself amplified, blowing through all his pipes, out from under his cape, a shuddery mix of moans and whistles, with parts like human voices, others like trumpets and other instruments, a park band, a whole orchestra combining to make the music he heard in his head. A big thing and we were all part of it. Souls rising, like beating wings, people singing and speaking out: a happy crowd that clapped and stomped, and I made my way to the altar, and Papa held me up to a microphone that dangled on a long cable from the steeple, and I did my parrot talk, imitating their strange tongue. I felt so light and free I almost managed to get out of my straps, walking on air. The whole church watched, in a hush. And we were like honored guests afterwards. They wanted to touch me. They said I had a holy ghost. And they weren't just making fun of me. There was a foodline at the altar rail. People were invited in, off the street. We were at the head of the line. They'd ushered us through. We hadn't eaten since the day before. Mama needed to sit, so they they put her on the other side of the serving counter with the ladies who were dishing out the food. People waited with their trays at the counter: a steam table with warming wells. We had a feast, with all the things to choose from: sizzling fries, chili bowls with white gravy made of drips, breaded stuff, meat pads, gritty corn mush, pepper pot pies and rinds and sausages, and fizzy drinks. It was an occasion, with party napkins. Someone had died and been reborn. A preacher had told the story, with gestures we could understand. People hugged us, like long lost friends. They said they'd missed us. They kept making me talk. It didn't matter what I said. They had a playground in back, with a swimming pool, kids splashing around in life vests or with kickboards, and when they dunked me, in my clothes, I discovered I could float, with just the air in my bones, letting myself be, in the body-warm water, freeing my arms and legs, like in my dreams when I slipped out of myself.

There were more and more pigeons. As the days went by, in towns and cow shows and auctions, warehouses, where there was always activity, furniture or machinery to be moved, fields with work that needed to be done, flea markets along the road where Papa sold his inventions, junkyards where we went for spare parts when we were having car trouble. And we had sightings and experiences. Once, powdery puffs blew on us in a cotton field. Like a blizzard of hot snow. We'd strayed down a side road and gotten out to feel the wind. There was a harvest moon, at twilight, with birds flying across its face. A vastness out there calling us. The radiance of a lit town over the rim of the horizon. Papa and Mama embraced, holding on to some memory, and drawing me up between them, almost weightless, as if I was no longer a burden to them, and I thought that if I could float I could also fly.

In towns without pigeons we made something else happen. We worked for several days in a fair. There was a country band, amusements: a maze, hay rides, and petting animals in a pen: goats and a freak donkey with male and female parts dangling. People arrived in pick-ups and campers. The performers with their equipment in trailers and cargo vans. We slept right there in the car, at a parking spot for cripples, it had a wheelchair sign, so they couldn't force us out. Papa pitched tents and sold tickets, wearing a funny hat. He bowed people through the gates. We rode a whirly with winding music. He made tweety birds and whistles for the kids and caught a lone pigeon in flight and sent if off with a message. Ladies on a box stage performed behind folding screens. There were spitting and yodeling contests, and cattle calls. Mama showed off a new dollar store parasol. A canopy of sunny colors over her milky beauty. Sometimes night ladies came for her. They recognized her from the way she carried herself. They took customers in the camper with the box stage. Kids played ghosts with pumpkin heads from a pumpkin patch. I played a string puppet on wobbly arms and legs. There were other disjointed kids, on crutches or in casts, because of an accident or disease, worse off than I was, some of them, but I had my mystery, I didn't forget that, I was that bird in Mama's song, born blind but with inner sight. A gang grabbed me and sent me down a slide into a sandbox, but I made my way back up some climbing bars, where I could twist and cling in ways they couldn't.

At another fair they had a head on a pole, with a beak and a feather crest. It was some kind of an Indian sign. And there was a birdman with a talking parrot on a perch in a wire loop. It looked like one of those birds smuggled in in bags. So he was on this side, too, he let me know. We did a parroty act together. Kids came and fed me crackers. They thought I was in the petting zoo. Other people bought me candied fruit and foamy drinks. And a balloon man pretended to hang me from his balloons. I saw a glassblower putting on a show. Dipping into a small furnace for molten drops, he puffed through a long pipe, and I realized it was Papa blowing hot bubbles and bottles.

Mama rode around with men at night. Sometimes she'd be gone for too long, they wouldn't bring her back, they couldn't be without her, or they'd make her get out in the middle of nowhere. Once she drove herself back in a man's car. We didn't know how she'd done it, she still couldn't drive, but she'd managed, just letting the car go, steering and braking, wide-eyed in the dark, with a drunk asleep at her side, and the next time we had to go out and look for her and we found her writhing and heaving, like when she was about to have a baby, in a ditch, where she'd hid when they tried to run over her.

Another time, when they'd been banging on our car and rocking it at a truck stop, and we couldn't tell who was after us, we drove all night, into a sky-splitting storm, our beams lighting up jumping spiders on the road, a cat-eyed owl on a post, snakes slithering across, a waterbelly cow that had come out of the brush to cool off in the breeze, crashing through the wire fence, and down into the bottom of the night, where we stopped for a while, as long as we dared, off the road, wrapped in each other, Mama's earthy smell and Papa's rough arms around us, his cape like the bark of an old tree, its fragrance in his breath, and when we couldn't get the car started a tow truck we called in hauled us into town raised high on our back wheels.

My hopes were up. Mama had lost her baby again. I'd make up for it, with my love and happiness. We'd be in full bloom. Papa would be someone, as he deserved, recognized at last for what he was. And maybe we'd find our home, instead of just imagining or remembering it: the place where we belonged, with people like us, and I'd have a life.

We came to an airport town. Windblown streets and parking lots, bleached white slabs of buildings like headstones. It was so hot that a drinking fountain spurted boiling water, even the hydrants steamed. We curbed the car and got out. Mama with her parasol spread wide. She'd come out of a heavy sleep. We hadn't been eating. We couldn't stop anywhere for long. And it kept us from being heat-sick. Papa hoisted me up on his back, his feet sinking into the tar pavement, which had blistered. He'd seen something, reflections in the dark windows of office buildings, like waves in melted glass. Across a junkyard where metal bushes grew, under a hum of high wires, in an industrial lot used as a dump, there was a rickety tower on stilts, the remains of a pigeon house, like the one he'd told me about in his past, in the old country Mama dreamed of, I recognized it right away, battered but still a wonder to see, with birds still homing in, flocking in and out of the holes with torn screens and the splinters of balconies. He'd been telling me about them and the messages they carried over long distances in their claws, beaks or rings on their legs, and a story he had, about how when they were shot down, or sometimes to begin with, if it was secret, they swallowed the message and carried it in their crop, which had to be slit to recover it. Life and death messages, they never failed. There was an old caretaker in a shack, and they got to talking, right off, in a kind of deaf and dumb language, shouting to be heard over the noise of the airplanes, which made me dizzy, and Mama standing there fainted for a moment, so fast she didn't fall, I felt her go and come back, and wings making wind, as birds beat down out of the high wires and caught Papa by the hair, as if to fly off with him.

I'd been needing help. I had cramps and spasms, as if a jumping jack had gotten into me. But I danced it off in a barn dance, after a market day. Papa whirled me around by my straps. The next day he bought me a pony ride, at a fun fair. Some long-haired kids rented them out. Bonita kids who traveled along secret trails with pick-up and drop-off points. They were going places, like us. Seeing sights and doing business. I got a bucking pony, mean as a wild donkey, but held it in a wide-legged grip, my bones taking on its shape, hanging on to its mane and withers.

Some days I couldn't get up. Though Papa rigged different supports for me, like love lady undies. But I crawled into the trunk. I had my body-shaped hole there. It felt like being underwater. I'd imagine I was drowning in a puddle. I'd fallen face down and couldn't turn over. It had happened to me once in the street, when my eyes failed me. I'd wake up writhing, my inner tube cushion suffocating me, my straps like claws around me, my bones on stiff hinges. But I'd remember who I was. And I'd hear Papa's spirit whistle.

On our way into another town, we stayed in a home on wheels, by a river. A place where they sold used homes and halves of homes and rented some to transients, wired and furnished, with cooling fans. There were vacancies and we had ourselves shown around, checking out the accommodations. They needed a maintenance man, and Papa fixed leaks and handled hot wires with his bare hands, he didn't mind what he did, always better than anyone else. There were some trees, and pigeons flew around. Trashy birds, people shot at them, but Papa sent them off storming like paper dragons. He pumped out clogged drains. Mama used the car for visitors. Parked under the trees in a bit of lamplight. The wisps of silvery white in her jet black hair shining like a halo. They called her Lady Love. A Big Mac man made the name up. Sometimes she was busy all night. The Big Mac man took pictures of her with a phone like Papa's. He had a photo room in his van. He said he could transmit the pictures to other phones. He gave her a calling card. I slept in a camp cot on our porch with wire netting. They called me Little Love. They liked to watch me get in and out of my straps. They couldn't figure out if I was a boy or a girl. We ate food bars and a man with boxes of bees in a farm truck gave me a honeycomb. It came with some bees, but they didn't sting me. We had a swamp cooler that drew water from the river and blew wet air through a fan. People had improvised and set up all around, with deck chairs and cooking grills, and everybody had something going. We'd been bumping into such people, who drove around with their businesses hitched in back, like the bee keeper, or living out of their trunks, job hunting or running from bad experiences. There was a gun salesman, and a health van that gave out needles, and a bearded tattoo artist cured pains with pin pricks and also did piercings, which he said released your inner self, and he'd tickle me with his fingertips as I went by, get me jumping in my body, and some kids would bounce me on a trampoline.

It was a life. Papa doing his pigeon sweeps, Mama playing Lady Love. We'd been seeing the Lady Love sign blinking over shuttered buildings off the road: a show lady that truckers worshiped, there were always rigs parked outside. We looked in one day, when we had to stop to let the overheated motor cool off. Mama had her calling card. A breathy dark place with rows of little bright screens like the faces of hand phones. They were coin movies of the Lady called videos. People sat in sweaty booths, watching. They could rent goggles for a different view. She also did a live show, behind a panel with peepholes, but she was sick that day, and they let Mama take her place, they'd looked up her picture, and there she was, in all her beauty, on a box stage, swimming in a watery light, like a fish girl we'd seen in an aquarium, the people at the peepholes watching her throw off her clothes in that way of hers, giving everything she had, and she repeated the show in other Lady Love houses. Papa would drop us off, on his way to some job he'd got wind of, and they'd take us in for the day, hiding me behind curtains from where I could sneak looks at everything that was going on. They were cigar-smoking businesswomen but with an eye for beauty, and people were asking for Mama, soon she was known at all the show places along the road. Truckers spread the word. We heard them over the radio, exchanging information, Papa would break into their talk line. There was even a Lady Love song, with cowboy music. And Papa was famous, too. They waited for us in towns with pigeons, we already had a following in some, and others made way for us, sometimes a police escort saw us through without letting us out of the car, because of the crowd. We slept in church lots or up some back way Papa had discovered from where we had a view of an outdoor movie screen that inspired us with its images. We washed up at truck stops. We'd checked out the best ones, also for quick eats. We'd remember where we'd kept money in a locker. We'd stop by and add some, or get some out. And we'd take a break in a motel with a pool where I could float and relieve my aches and cramps in body-warm water, my prickly skin sparkling in the underwater light, people keeping an eye on me. There'd be an ice machine, and sodas, and a double bed with a spring mattress, and a mirror where we looked glamorous, and Papa would be off doing night work, which could get him killed by hunters or a patrol, and Mama answered calls from the other rooms, from where she'd bring me presents, trinkets she'd picked up, buttons, hairpins, panties she'd found in a drawer, pretty things people had left behind, falsies, fake nails, and wearing them like jewels we'd go out and sit in some all-night snack bar, in friendly company, lady birds, a dreamy cashier blowing smoke rings, our movements pictured on a TV screen, Mama in her flimsy dress, which gave her a bloom the other ladies didn't have in their skinny jeans, and men with guns would come in and drop coins down her neckline, and once when she'd had some piercings done the men hung hooks and chains from the loops in her lips, nose and tongue, and candy sticks from my ears.

Sometimes we just walked up and down the strip. Late into the night. Papa was far away. A job hadn't worked out, he'd been called somewhere else. We couldn't sleep or breathe in our room or open the windows, we had to get out. And we were a sight. Mama in her airy dress. You saw right through it. I'd be pushing my walker, as if I was driving. Trucks blasted their horns at us. Great streaks of light, slashes of jaws that went by. Fireball signs lighting up, thunderbirds. Cars trailed us, honking, braking, then taking off, with a screech of tires. We had fun pretending Mama was a pick-up. I'd hide behind a ground sign and she'd thumb for a ride and when someone stopped I'd come out and scare them away. Once they'd pulled Mama halfway into the car, and when she backed out slamming the door her dress caught and she was dragged along until the skirt ripped off. A patrol saw it happen and gave us a lift back to our room. Two laughing cops who'd already met Mama. They were running a siren and a revolving light. They joked with Mama and they let me talk over their two-way radio.

We had new prospects. Job openings, in a growth area. We'd heard announcements. A big business town with fancy hotels in the outskirts. One of those high-rise wonders, out of nowhere. Skyscrapers mirroring the desert, loops of freeways, shopping centers, anything you could imagine. They were hiring at the hotels. Hospitality people, doormen, drivers, high-hat cooks. With great work conditions, housing, beautiful surroundings, landscaped gardens, night spots for love ladies. They didn't care where you came from. You didn't need work papers. We knew it was for us. It took us two days to get there. As fast a we could go, we almost reached the speed limit. On our last drop of gas. Papa had it all figured out. And we'd kept awake. We landed in a rental room, in a row of railway houses, got a loan from a lender nextdoor, and drove around. We had several interviews with managers. We parked in driveways and courtyards. Papa made an impression in his cape. They could see him ushering guests in and out. He got several offers he turned down. And they all wanted Mama.

We settled for an airport hotel with a terrace view. Inbound and outbound planes landing and taking off. And shady corridors with shops, meeting rooms, a beauty parlor, a pool in the inner courtyard, with tropical plants, a waterfall, a bar with cocktail waitresses. A dream of a place, just what we needed. There was some big conference going on, projections and displays of products, huddles in hallways, people closing sales, cutting deals in the bar. Papa was in the reception. And he drove an airport van with starlight inside, music and announcements. Mama was an escort, in a hostess gown. On call, at any time. She looked gorgeous and alluring. They didn't know what to do with me. But a dwarf bellboy dressed me in his uniform. I got a lot of tips without doing anything and we split them. He had a show-girl girl friend. She pretended we were in love. Her kisses left lipstick lips on me. And they let me ride with Papa in the van. Up next to him in cushiony comfort, with plush arm rests and neck support padding. It was called the Empire van. Besides the airport, he took parties to tourist spots, he had a map and soon knew all the places, a wildlife sanctuary, pit roasts, a space station, all sorts of entertainments, musicals, inspiring shows with lighting and sound effects, he acted them out for me when I wasn't allowed in. In his free time we rode a merry-go-round in a fairy tale park with talking animals, and even the rollercoaster, which was good for me, strapped in upside down, hanging on to my myself, or floating weightless in a freefall, between life and death, and Mama would have take-out food ready for us when we got home to our free housing, which was like one of the hotel rooms, with all the furnishings, in a service compound, and we'd do some more sightseeing on TV, on a travel channel, then we'd all take a shower together, whatever time of the day it was, and sleep for awhile in a cool air stream, till Mama was called out to keep someone company, or Papa to carry passengers around on their affairs. It could have lasted, except Papa wanted more. I was supposed to be going to school. A special school they sent me to, for kids with problems. I tried it out one day. Nice ladies took me in. They had play rooms, and an exercise room, and I got along with the kids, who had seizures and ticks and mouthed strange words, but none of them was like me.

Then Papa got another offer. So we picked up and we were off again in our speedster. Fitted out with new tires, we could afford the best, it started up with a big bang. Our fan going, hood wings and tail fins unfurled. And with our extra money we headed for a holiday town we'd seen advertised on posters, with amusements, magic shows, a wild west museum, a house of horrors with tunnels, slides and bounces, monster skulls in windows, zombies, witches, rattling skeletons, mummies hanging from nooses, wild laughs and screaming faces, happiness and madness, all mixed up together, as we rode through in seats on a moving belt: walking dead rising out of graves and coffins, like ghosts haunting you, jumping puppets like me, I was all over the place, running into myself and leaving myself behind. Mama and Papa, too, reflected in distorting mirrors, body and soul. Laughing our heads off at our aches and fears, as we liked to do. And then, a few miles down the road, we visited a shrine to a singer. They said he'd planned it himself, so he'd be remembered forever. His songs playing over a sound system. Running screen images of him. A monument, where he was buried. The tombstone had his footprint in cement. There was a trophy room, a meditation garden with a fountain, tree-lined walks, a memory wall with his words and sayings. We were on a guided visit. We went through the rooms. Closed places opening up for us. Some with valuables roped off. Displays of costumes, the singer's wax figure in a glass case. Mailboxes where you could leave messages. A gift shop that sold his autographed photo. It all fit us perfectly, as if it were about us. We signed a guest book. I was able to scrawl my name. We were so full of ourselves, some people asked us who we were. We let them take our picture. On the way out there was a mourning wall where famous people who'd visited had left their hand prints, and some were just our size.

We had more and more offers. Better conditions, bigger pay. Papa's phone kept ringing. He got so many calls he didn't bother to answer anymore. We took whatever came up. As long as we had a place to stay for a few nights. Weekend hotels that needed extra help. And it wasn't just for the money. It was the night life, the airport run. People flying in from everywhere. Visitors, vacationers. And others, workers, waiting in the dark along the road. Papa picked them up in the hotel van. They'd come up back paths or crosscountry. Sometimes they'd slide a door open and jump off along the way. Meantime, I watched after Mama. I took her window shopping in the hotel lobby. There were always a couple of shops with bright showwindows. I had to bathe and comb her first and help her dress. She wasn't herself some days. She'd be gone in the middle of the night without telling me. I'd wake up in the empty bed. She'd be gazing at herself in the hallway mirror. Once I found her swimming in the pool. I thought it was because we weren't allowed to use it at the same time as the guests, we had to sneak in at odd hours, when no one was around, but she was naked, with her clothes floating around her, they'd been ripped off, and floodlights came on, everyone saw her. We had to leave. And once during a storm we spent the night in an abandoned bus depot. A dark warehouse-like building with high windows, one of those out-of-the-way places where lives went on unnoticed, like us when we got around without attracting attention, we weren't the only ones. People smuggled in or broken down in the storm. There was already a crowd, with their bundles and suitcases.

Out of the wind and the downpour and floods. We'd heard the weather forecasts. Ramshackle trucks had pulled up, a converted schoolbus, campers. Travelers with their bedding. Some with nothing. Kids in rags, floppy babies. Runaway families and traffickers. All landed there for shelter, a stopover on their trip. I was so weak Papa had to carry me in. They made way for us, steaming on their damp mats. Winds blew through the high windows, noisy echoes amplified sounds and voices, even whispers, gestures casting shadows, and there were pigeons in the heights, you heard them whipping their wings as they came swooping down, clawing in the air.

We stayed all night while the storm raged, and we heard stories. All sorts of talk and sign language. Secrets these people let out loud. Traveling salesmen, preachers, bus riders, whatever they were. Some had been walking for weeks. Or they'd come in bins on trucks, railcars. All carrying things, messsages, hopes, songs, their money in moneybelts or sewn into their clothes, pockets, folds, pouches, body holes. Our kind of people, for a few hours. It did Mama good to be with them. They started small cooking fires with tricks they knew, snapping their fingers like matches over kindling, twigs or scraps of trash. Papa had a dollar store sparker. He made paper birds for the kids. They lit up like torches and flew off. We shared straw mats and bedrolls. Mama produced bags of snacks, as well as soaps and scents from hotel bathrooms, she'd been hoarding them. She drew people out. They'd been places, across the border. Back and forth from the other side. Running from jail, war, bad times, an earthquake or an epidemic. Other were just aimless wanderers, wayfarers. But they all knew about Mama, they'd seen her in lights, in some night spot or a Lady Love house. Some kids even had pictures of her. Cards showing naked ladies that they passed around. They fingered them like prayer cards, kissed them all over. They asked her which one was her. She laughed and wouldn't say. And she held crying kids to her. Kids with colics and lung diseases. She knew where to touch them. Like the market women used to do with me when I couldn't move or breathe. Sweet boy spots and girl spots that burned and brought me back to life. The air was thick with heavy breaths and smoke. The good air had all been sucked out the high windows in the storm. The pigeons flapped silently overhead like bats chasing bugs. But we were making people happy. I heard Mama singing to herself. And then suddenly she began to arch up and pant, deep in her body, and she was having another baby.

We rushed her to a hospital. Papa knew where to find it, I'd been there once for shots. Emergency people were waiting for her. Everyone knew who she was. In minutes they had her wired and tubed in. She'd lost a lot of blood, but Papa gave her all she needed. They had the same blood type, as I did, too. It was one of the things that made us different. Doctors and nurses crowded around her. She let them bend in and listen to her. They ran a curtain around her bed. They wouldn't let me in. They wanted to take me away. But Papa held me under his cape. We breathed on the curtain and made shadows so she could tell we were there. Then they moved her to a room with dividing panels for privacy. They could crank her up in bed. And other patients came to see her. They wheeled people in. Some came walking on their own, even from other wards, in their hospital gowns. They talked to her and listened. People you wouldn't have thought, shop lady types, workmen with job injuries, a barmaid Mama had once spoken to, a policeman who brought flowers. And cleaning people who looked in. Mama had a frail glow, in the pale light of the room. Her bottomless black eyes lidded, like when she wore her beauty mask against wrinkles. An ice cube melting on her dry lips. Her silvery halo of hair around her. In a while she looked drained, all her color gone, her veins showing through her skin, she was almost transparent. They said she was dead, and she could have been, but she wasn't, just asleep, with open eyes, under her lids, Papa and I were in touch with her the whole time, in our words and thoughts, which no one else understood. They pulled a white sheet over her head. Then we had her all to ourselves. The sheet billowing every time she breathed. She sat up, into Papa's arms. It was like when they did their loving, joined in a long sigh, and she'd be all milky afterwards, she'd let me taste it. There was one of those small graveyards out back. We could see it from the window. The hospital did its own burials for people without families. Plots neatly laid out, with lanes and unmarked graves. Another part had a lawn watered with sprinklers. Mama said she wanted to be there. She believed in life after death. Like she believed in life before birth. She said she'd still be with us. The burial was a do-it-yourself ceremony. You could buy flowers, a coffin in a funeral shop. You rented a shovel and dug a hole and hired a hand only if you needed one to help carry out the coffin.

You stopped at a chapel, where you put a coin in a slot and you got a voice that called out the name of the dead person and a prayer, and then organ music and a choir, somewhere on high, and you gave your own blessing, and Papa would be good at that. Mama wanted to go through with it. She wondered about people in the other life and whether they'd be like us. She said she'd be gone and back. But instead, while the doctors and nurses were busy with other patients, we walked her out, draped in the white sheet, which she threw off at the entrance, where Papa had left the car running and the doors open, and with a few people who'd noticed watching in silent awe, we drove away.

Papa had another inspiration. He decided to head out to the coast. There'd be jobs for sure, holiday hotels. It was the time of the year. We'd seen ads for a resort, an ocean city with a beachfront, offshore islands. A great bridge over a bay. Fresh winds, sea spray, high skies, everything we needed. We'd get Mama back to health, I'd be jumping in the waves. And we'd find work along the way. Odd jobs, in the oil towns. Staying in overnight places, maybe doing a show now and then.

We set out at first light. We'd slept in a field of blue flowers. Mama had their scent on her breath. She was still wearing her white hospital gown. It looked girlish and ethereal on her. The glare on the road would have blinded us, but we saw through the tinted window. A sun glowing in the distance. Like daylight in the middle of the night. It was another long drive, several hundred miles. We got out only for gas and when I had to stretch my joints. The sun came smashing down. The road boiled ahead, flat as a pancake. There were those endless cow pastures. Scrub and tumbleweed and dwarf bushes. We went through hay flying in the hot wind. And then another weather zone, along black oilfields with muddy ponds like dark inland lakes steaming in the haze. Pump heads working, drill towers, tent cities bristling with hot wires, construction trailers, storage tanks, container trucks, wellheads blowing firestorms. Then miles of heat waves. Dips in the road and, beyond, watery fields. A heavy breeze in which we could already smell salty ocean air that reached way inland. It got muggy in the evening light. We stopped to rest at an outdoor movie where they showed the same scenes we saw around us, as if the screen were just a big picture window. Papa sat me on his lap. We pretended I was driving. We were in the back row of cars, for an in-depth view. A search party, men and women dressed as men, came shining flashlights in the windows. Papa said they were looking for boat people. When he got out to open the trunk he was tall enough to cast his shadow on the screen. Then some ladies pulled up and parked next to us, in a stretch car. They had a bar right there in the car, with all the amenities, low lights and soft music. Mama, who'd slipped into a sheer dress, stayed with them after the movie, while Papa and I drove around watching for a ghost owl we'd seen flying off a tree with a great silent wing span, and when we picked her up she'd been laughing and drinking and she'd regained some of her life and joy.

We drove into the ocean air. A dazzling sun ahead. Ripples of clouds like ocean waves in the sky, oily marshes steaming on every side, the houses and trees seemed to be floating in pools of hot gas. It got sandy, windy, under a white-out sky, wiped out in the light. Spike-grass dunes broke through the turf. A reedy wet lowland seeped in, sunken watermeadows. We caught glimpses of the marshy sea. It was also the mouth of a river. By then it was getting dark again. A dim wheel of a moon spread a hazy light. The muggy wind blew in brine and fog. I swallowed mouthfuls of it, breaths of life. Mama had a salty glow. A kind of night-lit icing on her. And Papa the light of his vision. The ocean he was giving us. Called up out of his memory. Like the sound of a big silence stirring. We headed for the beach, across a long bridge, where pelicans plunged and flopped by, over the moonlit bay. Up the coast was a rocky point with a lighthouse. We came off the bridge into a palm-lined avenue. A short run with globe lamps and headlights, glittery hotel palaces. Then, out of the way, past the last building, a partly boarded sea front walk, and on to a stretch of packed sand, where we stopped in some tire tracks. A blast of night air hit us. Rips of light from the waves. Breakers far out, the high surf rolling in, blowing shreds of foam. Papa said it was where the boat people landed, in inlets bared among the rocks. You felt the sea swell, then the pull of the tide. There was a tarry smell, from offshore oil. Buried black fields out there. A steamy bog inland: sewage from pipes oozing in the marshes. You knew because of the marsh lights. But the open water had a skylit glimmer. Gulls and pelicans skimmed the waves. Surges of screeching sea birds, over the outer sand banks and barrier islands. A coast guard patrolled in jeeps and bigwheel bikes and buggies. They scattered some tall-neck birds, long-legged walkers. And bright night bugs jumped in pools around them. They came in the waves. We sat there in the car enjoying the breeze and the view. Moonlight and stars spilled across the sky. A tug went by in the bay, dragging a barge or an island, you couldn't tell. Papa said it was a dredge digging to deepen the bottom. He knew about everything that was going on. Before it got cold we went for a swim, in strangely buoyant water, hanging on to our clothes, which came off and began to drift away like seaweed, and we dried out on a cement slab that was still warm with sunlight.

The beach closed at night because of the landings: smugglers, the boat people. There were posted warnings. But we stayed on. No one bothered us. Parked on the cement slab, the remains of some building sunk in the undertow. A dune heaved beneath us like a beached animal. Some beach bums had lit a bonfire with driftwood. They were boiling fish bones in a pot, their hairy faces bristling. Gathered around the glow like wise men, transmitting thoughts. Papa got out to talk to them. We couldn't hear what they said, it was more gestures than words. Engaged in strange occupations, they made me blow on a seashell that sounded like a trumpet, and in another shell you could listen to the sea. They piled seaweed into the fire, and dry dung. They breathed the smoke in through reeds and drank their own piss out of a bottle.

We walked Mama back and forth. Barefoot along the edge of the water, foam sprinkling up our legs. I waddled along, almost without help, slapping my hands and feet down on the sand to keep from sinking, like some flatfoot birds I saw pecking at the surf. They could even stand on one leg. When we looked around, all sorts of activities were going on. Papa got into conversation with some men, roughneck types. Jobbers who'd do anything, like him. There was an oil tower out in the bay, all lit up, and a holiday hotel spreading music. Anchored somehow or on floaters. Papa picked up the sound. He had his phone, and I had my seashell. There was a chill in the air. Mama was shivering in her slip of a dress. We lit our own small fire on the cement platform. We didn't think of eating, we just wanted to gather around the light. Sparks jumped like fish tails when Papa spat into the flames. Other people, down the beach, were burning tires. Some fishermen drew in a heavy net. I felt smoked and salted in the spray. We listened to the offshore music. Bursts of it the wind brought in. It came from the hotel boat. There was also a radio station on a barge out there. On the other side of the border, Papa said. The border ran along the ocean bottom. The oil rig was over a huge sinkhole. A lit buoy halfway to the hotel was a transmitter. At low tide things emerged, stripped bare: jagged rocks, the hull of a sunken ship, an underwater wharf. Then a slow high tide began. We felt the surge. A sort or deaf roar at the bottom of the ocean. A beachcomber went by skimming the sand with a metal detector. I set it off, with clicks and pings. Like in one of those body searches in jail. Another tramp dug up tar balls, which he said were precious stones, and he saw a brightness in Mama as if she was wearing jewelry.

There was a shack nearby, on piles, where they hired people. Deck hands for boats, riggers. And a weather station with its vanes and aerials, taking in measurements, wind, rain, and doing forecasts, they sent signals, once they shot out a flare. Sometimes phones and radios weren't enough, we knew that from Papa. We'd seen windsocks along the road, big sound dishes, storm balloons. And now he invented a sort of weather bird for them. They were having trouble with their equipment. Some kind of atmospheric disturbance. And there were no messenger pigeons around, only some crazy gulls, so he made a sail out of Mama's lightweight parasol and sent it up like a kite on a long fuse, streaking the sky to where it caught some distant daylight or whatever it was, an otherworldly thing, breaking out from under the horizon.

A call came in. A supply boat with a spotlight and a loudspeaker. Papa had been expecting it. Miles away it had made itself heard. The prow bouncing over the breakers, bumper tires all around, it moored and tied up at a half-buried pier. It loaded and unloaded below-deck cargo with a winch. Fuel tanks and boxes, machinery. All the time with an announcement over the loudspeaker: ladies needed out on the oil rig. Lonely men at sea welcomed them with loving hearts. We hadn't noticed, but there were night ladies waiting in a parked car behind the employment shack. A flock that spilled out all at once, slamming doors, wearing life jackets. Sleek blondes, a couple of loud-mouthed black girls, strapped up in their girdles and uplifts, A Maria in a mermaid costume made of mosquito netting. A Mesias-type wheeler-dealer managed them. Mama was just herself. A gauzy shawl around her shoulders. But they wanted her. They got her past the hiring boss. I slipped through in the noise and confusion. They thought I was blind or dumb. Whatever Mama had told them. Out on the loading pier, they outfitted me in a life preserver. They said I was their mascot. Mama caught me in the boat, which heaved and swayed. The movement took us down below deck. Papa was off on another boat. They'd hired him at the offshore hotel. It had a casino, which meant a gambling palace. Mama would have done well there, too. But we'd decided we'd be happier on the high sea, under the open sky. The deck hands rolled up ropes, a whistle gave the signal. We shoved and backed off the pier, riding a swell, into the shadows, where the sea picked us up. In the dark except for a lamp on a mast and starlight. Wind and spray bursting through the cabin windows. We thumped along, out past the outer banks, breasting small waves, humps over ripples of foam with faint rims, then breakers raising mists like fireflies. I had my stomach up in my mouth but held on. Better than Mama, who looked like she'd swallowed her tongue. Several ladies took care of me. They hid me from the crew. A dark María wrapped herself around me. She said we'd be invisible. We blew grimy smoke out the chimney and dragged a dirty wake with an oilslick, and soon everyone was seasick, but by then they'd got a party going, out on deck, singing and retching overboard. Someone shot off a water cannon, which was hard to stop. Music drifted in on sound waves. It seemed to gather in the lamplight. A shiny black girl twisted in the coils of a rope, slick as a snake. I got going, too, stepping all over myself. They wheeled me around in my life preserver. And I showed off my beauty spots. Ear lobes and other tasty buds Mama said I had, good for love bites. She was drenched through her see-through dress. Queen of the night and the ocean, far and wide. The blaze of the deepwater rig ahead, big as a city block. A looming tower somehow anchored in the seabed. On pilings or floats and some kind of stabilizers on all sides with motors to keep it in place. It must have had deep weights. Still, it seemed to sway. Up and down on its platform, as we came heaving and hooks caught us and pulled us in. The ladies let themselves be hoisted in a hanging cage on pulleys that raised them along a metal shaft, into the higher reaches. Like a great pump drawing us up, through floors made of grates. I was a pile of bones, hips and shoulder blades. At first dropping out of myself, but then light as air. And Mama a night bird soaring. A clanging, deafening noise all around, from turbines, generators, wind and sea powers blowing. We knew Papa was behind it somehow. He must have found some way to come with us. He could be any one of those roustabouts we saw in hard hats and goggles, hammering, drilling, pounding on hot metal, it was one of his great acts. There were several floors, bridges we climbed, when we got out of the cage, metal staircases, with long falls, blinding lights in our faces, pits of darkness below, till we reached a living area. I got all the way up on my own, and Mama with a lot of helping hands. They gave us earplugs for the noise, safety glasses against sparks, hard hats, steel-toed boots, strong as braces. We had a bunk in a bunk room. A locker where we hung our things. Some ladies were already splashing in a shower, swishing around and fixing up in mirrors, busts and crests. Half drunk with the sea sway and wild as birds, drinking flames out of flasks, as jukebox music started up in the recreation room, and Mama a goddess among them, and they said I was their lucky star.

We never slept all night. After freshening and powdering up. We braved the noise and seesawing depths. Stepping through lights, music, in a while we had our sea legs, as Mama said. It was easy for me, like in my dreams. And she carried herself in that way she had, so whatever happened, people were gracious to her. The party was in a recreation room. There was a pool table and a TV with built-in shows and others captured in dishes and antennas that pointed in every direction. The men came in in shifts. They worked, slept and ate like that. Playing hard, in their big risk world, giving out their lives and taking them back during breaks. The ladies going fast with them. Dressing and undressing in the bunk rooms, pulling the men in. Sometimes out of turn, any minute they had off from their rounds and watches. Joy ladies, love ladies, each doing her thing. Wonders of movements and body beautiful things, everything I dreamed of. At moments I even thought it was me doing them, dropping out of my clothes and straps. The ladies caught me writhing and laughed and said I was giving them ideas. A man noticed I bit my nails. We'd been playing hands on the pool table. He said it was the sign of a passionate nature. He'd just come in from the wind. He was going to teach me frog talk. He looked weatherbeaten, like Papa. I wanted to give him something precious. He wouldn't take a kiss, but I licked salt off his face. And I saw Mama letting them drink from her. Lying wide open to them: her mouth, her eyes and armpits, her love lips in the sweetest place they'd ever seen, they wanted to taste everything. They dandied up for her, changing out of their work clothes into night glow shirts. They sprayed on after-shaves and hair glaze. A man with a prickly head put on a fancy mop. Another sported dentures with gold and silver teeth. He said he'd had the real ones pulled so he wouldn't ever need a dentist while he was out at sea. They wore tattoos all over their bodies. They'd gone through great pain for them. They'd been wrestlers and carnival performers. Jailbirds, with gunshot or stab wounds. Blowhards made up stories. And Mama heard them out. It didn't matter what they said. They were all in a sweat over her. I had my admirers, too. An underwater air washed up from the sea, and I swam in it, showing off my beauty spots. Hands clutched at me, and I slipped through them. There was a great moment when a helicopter landed on us. Up on top, out of the sky, on a landing pad where we'd gone to watch, a blaze of light came down, with a blast of wind that nearly blew us away, and men reached out the door and picked up the sick and wounded in fights or work accidents, and a man who was raving, who'd lost his mind in the night light that never went out, and they were off again, drawing in a tide that almost pulled us up after them.

In the morning we were still going. There were the same work shifts and breaks, only with sunlight instead of the night lights blocking out the dark.

Tired, worn men unwinding. They kept Mama busy. They couldn't do without her. In between, we took short naps. Wherever we were: on a deck chair, in a hammock. We'd learned to sleep with an eye open. A man who chased birds off the decks wanted to string me up in a rope net. He'd seen me being sick. He said I'd hang without swaying. But I was getting my exercise catching my balance. I chewed and spat out gum with the men, and they'd give me a lift to another level, where they were doing maintenance, hanging overboard on slings, taking calls and signals, I saw it all. They mopped, painted, sand-blasted, welded pipes, fought rust with needle guns, checked for fires with fire-extinguishers. The great pump and life-supporting machinery going all the time. Blowing hot as a furnace or flushing out. Every now and then the deafening windspan of sound of the helicopter landing on its pad, people jumping out. Cranes swung pipes across metal decks. A clanging and clashing everywhere. The elevator hoist raised supplies from barges in baskets and pods. Everything was so hot you couldn't touch it. And a spark could light it and blow us up. Men swung on high masts or wires. And down a long drop, wherever you looked, through the grate floor, you saw all the way to the sea. You heard it beating and billowing down there. And the cries of sea birds, bursting through the other sounds. At times the rig was like a huge bird cage, full of screeching gulls, pelicans, terns diving and fishing in the waste emptied out into the churning water. We ate all the time, in a mess room. Line-up style, like in the food palaces. Whole meal stuff, dried, frozen in trays, and bubbly cooler water, all packaged and clean, no drugs or booze. They made wads in their cheeks. Supposedly they were steaks and seafood. They slept it off in the bunk rooms. Four bunks to a room. I had a berth I could climb out of the back way. And I got around, up and down grates, railings, monkey bars. I seemed to have always lived there. A seaborne, skyborne life in me. I chatted with the birds. I could have jumped off and flown with them. I had views everywhere. Hidden places, too, till they showed up on TV screens. There was an exercise room with weights and a moving walk. Coin machines rang and gave out chews and, smokes, rubbers, beauty items for the ladies. Sewage tanks flushed and drained waste into the sea. A water plant made drinking water out of salt water. It sounded like a pipe organ. I hung on and clambered up rungs, to an air-conditioned lookout with a glass dome, like a bell jar, but wrapped in steel webbing. A kind of space ship suspended there. Papa could have imagined it. A far-sighted eye opened in the web and scanned the sky. And there were private places where you could be with yourself. Chemical toilets that were little think tanks. You sat on the can just listening and being. I felt the world banging, my brain boiling. Frogmen and deep sea divers swam around below, checking pumps and motors, doing inspections and repairs. In wetsuits and masks with windows, helmets, like robots with breathing tubes. Oil drums knocked around them. Logs and floaters like coffins. It got dark early. Lights blazed again. Hot fires up and down cables. Mama was busy, and I'd been needing a helping hand, and the bird man with the rope net caught me in the net and lowered me to where I skimmed the surface of the water. There was another man down there, on an inflatable raft, in a spotlight, shouting, waving to get the light off his face. Boat people, they said, sunk off the coast, a survivor. He wouldn't speak when they hoisted him on a man-lift, shivering in a life preserver, but we did hand talk, with gestures I understood, because they were like Papa's.

Night and day, it went on. Life work and fun and music in the break room. The ladies in style, playing sweethearts, loves, call girls, waiting on the men, broken hearts crying over them, mothering them, they could do anything, mad passion, lost love. Changing in and out of costumes. Goodtime girls, loving wives, whatever was needed. Fresh out of the mists of a shower, or in busty girdles and beauty masks. They had their acts and laughs. I saw one step out of a wetsuit. She said she was being born in a seashell. It was like when I'd wriggled out of the cast they'd meant to trap me in at the hospital. Mama sang bosomy songs. She wore a gauzy dress or a fishnet body stocking with starfish. She did sighs and joys, exchanging clothes with the other ladies. We had our locker in the change room. I slept in there for a while. It was on our second afternoon. They'd shut me in expecting bad weather, but Mama got me out. She sang a dove song for me. Hooing and cooing in her throat. We were thinking of Papa. Hoping he was well. As the day wore down, bursts of ocean spray reached us. We sat up on a high deck, over the sea. Drinking coffee to stay awake, looking out. There were other rigs out in the bay, lit up, into the sky. I had a hazy view of them. One was a launching pad for a rocket, someone had told us. It was like a big fiesta tower. You felt the energy exploding. Fires flashing up cables, a huge power grid. Solar panels and moon panels like flap wings charging circuits, and other things we'd been hearing about in the men's talk. All like Papa's inventions, he'd foreseen it all. Space dust fell on us, the pumps and motors raised us high, swaying to the music of pipes and cables. Seabirds circled overhead and below. We leaned over the handrail, into the glow of the sea. Shadowy fish swam just below the surface, along the waterline. I could just make them out. Sharks, rays winging by. Plunging and flying fish. Men swam around with them, in deep sea diving suits, some in cages, looking for the boat man, who'd jumped back in and gotten away. I'd known he'd do it because of his gestures. Even when they had him tied up, he was working himself free, like one of those contortionists in fiesta fairs twisting out of ropes and chains, the way I did, shifting my bones, I could have jumped in after him. The swimmers made oily streaks, their underwater shapes in phosphorescent bug light. Several ladies had shed their clothes and dived in with the men, wearing flippers and fins, doing a bathing beauty show. They were calling out to Mama, and soon she was down there, swimming in her fishnet: the beauty queen, in all her glory. And the bird man, laughing with some other men, caught me and dropped me in his rope net, down the length of the tower, into the waves, and on down and under, sinking so fast it cut off my breath, so I didn't drown, but came back up treading water when he fished me out of the deep.

They gave us a big send-off. Flares, fire hoses, wellwishers waving, and we rode the breakers all the way back in the supply boat, our whistle hooting, soaked in spray. The ladies still in a happy mood, yawning and stretching into the morning air. Several tongue-kissing, to wash the men away, they said. With big-hearted embraces for me. Papa was already back, waiting on shore, with people wrapped in his cape, just off a flat-bottom barge that had grounded. It turned out he hadn't been on the music island or the holiday hotel but bringing in boat people. His cape looked ragged and torn, some pockets ripped out, but he could still fit everyone into it. People who didn't show their faces, but they kissed Mama's hands, and we carried several with us in the car, crouched in back and in the trunk, slowing at wayside stops for them to jump off, at a sign with an electric Indian doing a war dance, which meant money games, where there was always employment, another at a whale-shaped eatery blowing kitchen smoke out its blowhole, and the rest into the woods.

Then we ran into some Bonita people. We'd been seeing them in regular jobs, at Big Macs and Star stations, when they ventured out of hiding, coming and going across the border, a step ahead of patrols, staying on as long as they could, like us, and Papa even knew some of them, from jail. It came out in the talk: times when they'd been rounded up. Nights when we'd thought he was working, he'd been locked up somewhere. And he hadn't told us: how it had once taken several men to hold him down, at a border outpost. And how he'd gotten away, disguised as a repair man, or digging through a tunnel. There was even a rumor he'd bent the bars of his cell with his bare hands. Another time he'd set himself on fire as a protest. So they welcomed us like heroes, in our elegant car. They called Papa don: a great man you looked up to. Like one of those Mesias men who managed several ladies. And Mama was family. She belonged to everyone. Smothered in hugs and lipstick kisses. They'd moved into a row of boxes with doors, just off the road. Storage sheds, where people left their possessions or supplies when they moved on, for others who came by later. They'd broken in several doors and camped there. Vans and trucks parked in a ditch behind. A real settlement, even if they had to pick up and leave the next day. Day laborers, field hands, cleaning crews, hotel drivers, service people, dishwashers. Kicked out of some job or beaten up, or just lost and wandering. They'd ended up there, gathered around themselves. Finding things and handing them down when they left. Their whole lives with them. Their laundry strung on a wire fence. They had a mobile kitchen with camp stoves, pots of beans boiling, and hot drinks on their breaths, just like back in the markets, we felt at home, at least for a few days. We borrowed a shed and pallets. I played with the kids, their stones and sticks games. They were as scrawny as me, and hungry, like when I used to eat roots and dirt. And the women loved to hold and touch me, because of the baby body they said I still had, and to listen to Mama, who sang to herself all the time, even when you couldn't hear her. They seated her on an upholstered car seat they'd installed in our door, under a parasol, fanned her when she seemed faint. Now that they had her, they held on to her if she tried to get up, so hard their nails left scratches on her, they kept pleading:

"Don't go". They patted and pinched her cheeks to bring some color back, she wasn't wearing any, just her moony beauty. And they took care of Papa, too. They sewed and patched his torn cape, washed his cracked feet. So glad to have us there with them, offering us their bottomless resources of love and help. It was a great soul time. All of us swept up in it. Love ladies chanted and lit candles. They had prayer cards with saints and a Lady Liberty with her crown and torch. Hot gushes sounded when people relieved themselves in the bushes. Sleepers gasping, bodies rolling over, mourners weeping and wailing. More people came out of hiding in the dark. Gypsy workers who flew like birds with the seasons. They had a music band, a peso shop, a medicine van, all set up right there with them. The band played brooding music. A brassy serenade, for Mama. She was pale, absent again, and shivering. In a cold glow, instead of her milky moonlight. We knew we were losing her, into the next life that she believed in. Even with Papa inside her she couldn't stay warm. When I held on to her in one of my fevers, I felt her slipping away. I knew she'd be all right, in that place she dreamed of, with people like us, so we were happy for her. The band had violins and strung gourds and guitars, but only the winds played, over a low drumbeat. A fiesta band doing funeral music. It sounded like a parade, but with slow marchers dragging their feet. They had small mouth instruments, not the usual big brass: tiny pan pipes, harmonicas. Held in their teeth or cheeks. One man played a mouth harp, placed sideways along his teeth, shaping the sound with his lips, tongue and throat, he hummed and twanged, hollowing out his cheeks, a hand cupped over his mouth, as if blowing to keep a small flame going. Others made a buzz or a drone, just sounding their voices. There were finger-size bone flutes made of relics. Dug out of the graves of those lost along the way. A miracle man sold them. Papa joined in on a reed pipe with a spiderweb membrane, his spirit whistle. I did my creaky bone sounds. And it caught on, everyone made muffled body noises, they clapped their palms in dull thuds, beat on their bellies, blew like bellows, all their aching joints making music, laughing jaws, broken heartbeats, a joyful pain, and all for Mama. She'd faded in our arms. Reminding us she'd still be with us in the next world. They were washing and dressing her. Laid out in one of the sheds. Funeral ladies instead of joy ladies, but it was just like when she was prettying up in a love house. Powdered and scented and touched up, with her own colors, out of her beauty kit, to show off her jewelry, her sweet-tipped breasts and lips that had left a taste on so many tongues. They'd snipped locks of hair from her and shreds of clothing for keepsakes. She was singing her bird songs. I could hear them, under her breath: the one about the blind bird, and the love bird, and the bird of sleep. The band played its mouth organ music. I did a parroty song and dance for her, as if I was clawing my way around a ring. She'd given me a last kiss. Like a small precious stone pursed on her lips. A family jewel she'd been saving for me. The one I thought she'd sold. She lay there all night, glowing. Our headlights shining on her. Papa had pointed the car at her. He wanted her in a bright light. He kept the motor running, siphoning gas in mouthfuls from a stranded truck. She wore a frilly dress, like a bride, and she had the organ music, mourners in fineries like night ladies, the best of everything. A cross made of live branches the burial people said would flower, watered with our tears. There was a burial plot, one of those off-the-road graveyards, in dry brush behind the ditch where the cars were parked, and Papa carried her out, wrapped in his cape, his tremendous frame shuddering over her, and dragging me after him, on my knees and elbows because I couldn't walk, weepers and wailers helping me, and he lowered her into a body-size hole he'd dug through bone-hard soil. She hadn't wanted a coffin, so she could come back, and her shape kept showing through the clods that fell on her, as if she was rising up out of the ground, and our whole beings with her, in a sudden darkness Papa called down from the sky, as they filled in the hole, and we planted the live cross, and some pigeons from the sheds landed on it.

We kept our headlights on, into the next town, where there was a spectacular games arcade, a long gallery Mama liked to stroll through, while Papa played the machines. They had betting games and bright hot screens that took you on car races, airplane flights to fantastic places, and a Lady Liberty, with her crown of stars, which lit up like a halo when you put a coin in her slot, and she clicked and whirred, as if about to say something, and gave out her picture. She was just putting on her starry show when we arrived. Her torch giving out rainbow beams, she drew us into her radiance. I could see Mama with her parasol. Drifting by, as if walking on water. Everyone around us wanted to listen to her and have her picture. They dropped coins into her like wishes. Some people cheated with slugs, flattened bottle caps, all sorts of clinkers, anything to get her attention, and when she broke down they shook her and banged on her, and before they could get hold of a repairman Papa pulled tools out of his cape, keys and wrenches, and worked feverishly on her till he got her going again, the way he did with me on mornings when I'd be lying awake but couldn't move.

We saw more Bonita people the following days. Crop pickers flapping like scarecrows in the fields, service people out of vans, lined up in their baggy clothes with tools and lunch pails along a street in a town, waiting for work, crews in bright vests, with pokers and plastic bags, collecting litter along the highway. Picked up in trucks to do a job, then thrown by the road. Others, we heard, dropped back across the border. What saved us was Papa's world size. His always being somewhere else and more than himself. Wherever it was and whatever he'd done, the immensity was in him. He'd go into a bar and arm-wrestle anyone down, drunk or sober. They'd get him to make figures in the air, pull out flying papers, snap springs to trap bugs. He dangled wiry puppets, cut sculptures out of corks. You felt they meant bigger things, he could have walked a tightrope, swung from a perch like an aerialist in a circus. He played musical instruments, made glasses sing running a finger along the rim. He didn't care whether they laughed or threw money at him, he was above it all, sailing out ahead, seeing birds on lighted wings. And he was proud of me and the things I could do, like change shapes inside my skin, or my blind and dumb act, or my parrot talk, when I clowned and imitated people, as if guessing their thoughts. Sometimes he talked through me, like a ventriloquist. We were very close those days, thinking of Mama. I'd gone mad one night and tried to gouge out my eyes and bite off my tongue. My bone pains tearing me apart. But he said it was my life force breaking through. And he had his shadow being in another world. They couldn't take that from us: our other selves or bodies moving in us. Something inside us but beyond us. He did shows of strength. He'd hold a chair in his teeth or punch out an airhole. Once there was a drinking contest. In a sagebrush cowboy bar. Seasoned ranch hands tossing their heads back. He put down one shot of firewater after another. Everyone was boiling, he kept cool, sweating it out. After about twenty drinks, I'd lost count, he was just a bit stiff when he got off the bar stool. We hadn't eaten, we'd been so busy we'd forgotten about food. He didn't need anything. And I'd had a gassy soda. It made me talk. He stood on a table to hold up the roof. People made a joke of it, they asked him whether it was true he'd once raised a car off the ground to rescue someone trapped underneath, then they watched him push our car at a run out on to the road to get it started, with me at the wheel. It gave us an air: we were artists, performers. Mama had always said so. No one knew about our down days, when I'd let go and Papa had to get me out of my bindings and wash me up in some dirty service station bathroom where they hadn't wanted to let us in, or he'd struggle through the day bent under the weight of memories he wouldn't tell me about, calling for people I'd never heard of. Another time I was half asleep at the bar. I'd been talking my head off, and they gave me something to drink, and I couldn't move my arms or legs, and meantime Papa, answering a call, staggered out the door and lay down across the road, and a pick-up ran over him, with loud thumps of tires. But he pulled himself up unhurt, just wavering a little when he walked.

Sometimes he couldn't take me on a job, he left me in a safe house with some kind people, or ladies. They all remembered Mama. They spoke about her as if she was still there. Some had pictures of her. Prettied up like a saint, but you could still recognize her. It upset Papa, who'd drive off without turning back. Once a trailer home put me up. A mission family with a lot of hand-me-down clothes. Big fat joyful people, angels in aprons. They'd collected used toys and had a yard with play things, swings, slides. It was a way of life with them. They took in stray kids, before they fell into the wrong hands, they said. Some were crazy kids or cripples, like Bandera kids. Nobody else knew what to do with them. They gave them love and care, got them up on splints and crutches. They'd rescued kids who were being bought and sold, like smuggled birds. They taught the girls to be lady-like. Some were Bonita kids who'd come across on their own or escaped when their families were sent back. They put funny face stickers on them. A special kind that left its image on the skin when it was peeled off. They outfitted me with light braces that were handier than my walker. Papa was shaking when he left me. It was a tremor that came over him, since his accident, driving or walking.

He said it would soon be gone. And I was shivery and hungry. So they fed me, wearing a bib, healthy things of theirs, corn flakes and bacon bits, through my chattery teeth, minced meat paddies, sweet sodas that made me sick. It wasn't Mama's milky breath when she fed me out of her mouth, I couldn't swallow. But I was good at finding street food. When I got myself together, I roamed with the Bonita kids, picking through the trash cans in an alley behind a supermarket. Among the chewed-up boxes there was overripe stuff thrown out, fruit and vegetables, that tasted as rich and juicy as in the markets on the other side. We flew around, with bird calls, whenever an unmarked patrol nosed up the alley. It always caught someone and almost got me one time when I fell over myself, but Papa, who'd made a pile on a bet in a bar, was waiting for me around the corner in our car, and we got away.

Days later, on a stretch of empty road, we spotted a Lady Love house. One of Mama's places, with its showgirl sign. There weren't many left, they'd been closing down, we'd heard it over the radio, and we hadn't dared stop at another one we'd seen, because of the police cruisers parked outside, which made this one all the more inviting. Shuttered under its blinking sign, shadowy and secluded. It was an emergency. Papa had to be off alone. He'd been seeing something, way out. His bones racking to get going. He'd spoken to some business people, they'd made promises. I'd heard him snoring at the wheel: sleep-talking to himself. And the house was a good place to leave me. The ladies were waiting. He'd phoned or sent a signal. It was a quiet time of the day, with only a few videos working. They let me watch and perform some of the movements. They called me Little Lady. They said I looked just like Mama. When they were making up they asked me for my beauty secrets. I was there for a day and a night. You couldn't tell day from night in the twilight. Just times when it got busier and others to lazy along, gazing at yourself in the screens like watery mirrors. I slept and woke up everywhere. I couldn't show myself when there were customers in the room, but when no one was around I got out on to the sweaty box stage, in the hot spotlight, behind the panel with the peepholes, and since there was no closing time there might still be someone watching, and I felt gleaming eyes on me and I twisted out of my straps, the way I'd seen Mama do when she was performing, and I wasn't ashamed of myself or the crooked bones sticking though my skin, because I was baring my inner beauty.

We'd made some money but lost our money belt and emptied all our lockers in truck stops, so Papa did a few pigeon sweeps in towns where we hadn't been before. Wherever there were messenger pigeons flying around, from parks or buildings, before they could pick us up for creating a disturbance, he called them down, blowing on his spirit whistle, and waved them away.

Then one day he invented something new: he ended the pigeon sweep bent double over himself, as if bowing to applause, dropped on his knees, and with a lunge stretched out flat on his face, bumping his forehead on the ground, and held out a flop hat. So I knew for certain what I'd always suspected: that he was a beggar. In his other world and in this one, too. But in a big way, even mightier than I'd imagined, a great gaunt figure of life and longing.

It was one of those towns with no one in the streets, once you got through the outlying miles of parking lots, but suddenly everyone came out to look. He seemed to catch all the store lights. He did it for me: I'd been sleepwalking, without my straps or braces, and without being asleep. Not always but some days. Buoyant, like when I'd swum in the ocean. Kicking my legs out, down the streets. As if I knew where I was going and how to get there. While he did his pigeon sweep, I'd move on, ahead of him. Out of my crabby walk, toward some edge but without going over it. He followed me, careful not to to wake me up. Asking me where I was and encouraging me, telling me I'd get there. Like Mama when she used to say my time would come. Sometimes I could keep it up for a while. Even if I tripped and fell, because I couldn't make out where I was going, I got myself up and went on. And that was what I was doing when I felt him lagging behind me and turned to see him go down flat on the sidewalk. So overcome that he had to be helped to his feet by passers-by, hands on every side holding him up respectfully. Quakes and tremors running though him: he hadn't eaten since Mama's death. He said it kept his mind clear. And it brought in quantities of laughs and money and gave us a new inner strength as we withdrew to our double-parked car, which had been blocking traffic, and wrapped in his lordly cape we drove through the crowd at a stately pace. It was just us and life. Big as fate. And we repeated the show in several towns. Whenever we needed to buy gas. We'd park at the far end of town, backtrack on foot up the main street, waiting for favorable conditions, then strike out, making our great airwave as Papa went down on his face under his cape and staggered up again. They didn't stop us when they saw the agonies we were going through, dragging our bones with us. Papa starved and racked by pains as bad as mine. Even if there weren't any pigeons, he'd pull the world down on him, sprawled on the pavement, with his hat out. So fast, it was as if he'd landed out of the sky, casting his long shadow. I shambled along, on all fours. Tied up in my tightening knots. Sometimes I had my walker. I'd wheel it into someone or off the curb. If we didn't like a town we coursed through it, they'd be expecting us at the next one. Our fame had spread. Everybody knew us. We snarled traffic, crowds gathered. They'd help Papa along. I'd let go of my walker and take some wayward steps, as if about to go off an edge. We'd cross the street against the light. We were such an attraction they didn't want us to leave. In one town they slashed our tires. We slept in the salvage yard, where Papa found spares and did repairs. A whiskered man called Rojas ran the place. When he heard us talk he wouldn't let us pay. He hugged me and became emotional. He'd known Mama as a Maria. He made sparks with Papa under the hood till they got the motor running, and we were off with the radio and the dashboard fan going full blast.

On a big day, after several long bows, we ended up in the park with some bums on benches. They made body-shaped places for us: a home out under the stars. Just in time, because it was getting cold. They gathered at nightfall, with frosty breaths. Like hairy bush people, out of their lairs. Lost souls transmitting thoughts that brought them together, mumbling and doing fidgety things. Some with a deep bow like Papa's, a solemn greeting, as survivors who'd made it through another day. The park lamps had been smashed. All the energy of the town used up. Only a faint haze left, its chill spreading. They made light by burning twigs and leaves, anything they could find, trash, weeds, striking sparks with their bony nails like claws. Others with pocket flashlights or glow fingers, whatever they had, or by simply being there, giving out body heat. They ate out of cans or paper bags. Food scraps or stuff they'd hoarded. It was a sort of vigil. Waiting to see who'd get there. Anxious but pretending they didn't care. We understood their language. Vagrants of all sorts, shifting and moving about, some with their bedding, folding chairs, mattress rolls, clothes bags, scattered on the grass, others just passing through, long-distance walkers carrying their bundles of rags. We'd seen them along the roads and scavenging in alleys, sleeping under cars in the rain. They came dragging their feet, making their glow on the paved paths, like slugs leaving a slimy moonlit trail. Warily, picking their way where they'd been mugged or beaten, looking out for the ones that were missing, thrown out somewhere, they went around poking a foot at bodies stretched under the trees, tipping them over to find out if they were still alive.

We spent a few nights with them. And with other bums in other towns. Great enlightened nights.

Muffled up in the cold. I'd had to get a coat in a
church giveaway, and thick panties to make diapers,
with layers of cloth padding. They kept me steaming
hot. The bums wore draughty wraps and cloaks.
Hoods, cheesy socks, shoes stuffed with newspaper,
misshapen sizes of clothes in which they did clownish
things. One played the mystery man with me. He had
his head in a paper bag with airholes. He'd pull the
bag off, baring black teeth. Another was electric and
gave me a shock when he touched me. They could
kiss or kill you on an impulse. You felt it surging in
them. A kindness with a murderous smile. Papa was a
courtly presence in a silvery sun foil he wore over his
cape. He'd ripped it out of a parked car. They shared
food and passed pissy drinks around. Whatever got
them going, chewing on their lips, lumpy tongues.
Their voices like background noise in a radio. All of
them tuned in, passing on information about handout
houses and soup kitchens. One rubbed a bottle and
listened to faraway sounds, holding it like a seashell
to his ear. A smoker blew white ashes: snowflakes that
fell on him like spiderwebs. A showman trapped a bat
with his cape. Gone in a sort of absentmindedness.
They spoke of their travels, good and bad places
they'd been, and old times, other places. One carried
on about a home country. He called it the old world.
He spoke with an accent. And others, too, in a strange
language, like Papa when he was lost in his memories.
They sounded just like him. They borrowed or stole
things from each other, dentures or glasses, they
took turns using them, wiped or licked them clean.
They exchanged mismatched gloves and shoes,
tied each other's shoelaces, emptied each other's

pockets. They all had things to show: coupons, store samples, bus tickets, pills and soap flakes, a bubble or ice cube that didn't melt, dead bugs, odd gadgets, rags of old bandages, the kinds of things Papa made into toys and inventions, linty mush, stringy hair, thumbed family photos. A bum had pictures of his kids, or maybe grandchildren, there were so many of them, and he knew all their names and birthdays, he presented them to me, one by one. Another tried to get me to reach through a hole in his pocket and grab a hairy ball. There was a business bum who made loans. He said everyone owed him an eye or a tooth. All sorts of characters turned up. Out of jails and death camps, Papa said. Voyagers, stopping for a moment on their global wanderings. They came for company. Messy drunks, some of them, fighting off bug-infested nightmares, others neat and picky, ate out of their own tin cups and spoons, one of them even kept his napkin in a ring and tied it on like a bib. Huddled there with hacking coughs, noisy shifting bones, scraggly beards, seeing things, blowing snots through their fingers. And with incredible skills, like threading a needle to sew on a button or aiming a gob of spit. They knew how to bundle up to keep warm and shiver to cool off. They wore earmuffs, wild manes. A bald bum wore a hairpiece like a scalp. He said he'd inherited it. And they discussed their travel plans. One was going to catch a plane home. He said he'd been gone too long. Another had landed in a space ship and was waiting for the next one to take him back. And another was on a hunger strike, protesting because they were going to deport him. So weak and lightheaded he had visions. He shouted and

writhed in his sleep, like me when I dreamed I was
buried alive. There was a time traveler. He said he
was in his afterlife. Papa knew what they meant. He
was also out somewhere, on swallows of some hot
brew. He still hadn't eaten, he didn't touch anything,
except to taste it to see if it was all right for me, he'd
take a bite and spit it out. He caught and shaped a
flame that floated by, blew figures out of it, ashes that
flew up with wings. Once he brought down pigeons
from the trees. Dark messengers like garbage birds,
sitting on the bare branches they'd killed with their
droppings. He aimed high and wide, a quick sweep,
because if a bum caught one he plucked it and ate it,
but they landed on our shoulders, tangled in our hair,
beating their wings in our faces, and he held on to me
so they wouldn't carry me away.

We drove on, watching for pigeons along the road.
The car bucking and stalling, choking up, after being
battered in a tow lot. But Papa fed it firewater, out of
a gallon bottle he'd been drinking from. He still took
calls on his hand phone. Though he hadn't charged
it for months, and it wouldn't plug into the lighter
anymore, it worked anyway. Ads and announcements,
radio voices came in. Sometimes a disembodied song.
We thought it was Mama trying to get through. Signs
streaked by the windows, flash messages. Mailboxes,
birdhouses, windsocks. We stopped in truck stops to
check our lockers. Mama used to leave a card or a
token inside for the next person, so they'd remember
us, in case we didn't come back, and they'd all
been opened. In the bar there'd be someone who'd
known her. Macs, traffickers, a gambler who called
her Lady Luck. A night lady who talked with spirits

said she'd had word from her. And a trucker drew
her face on a napkin. It was the same everywhere.
Street kids trailed us in towns, tripped us up during
our show. Once Papa landed hard and skinned his
knees and hands but got up with a skeleton-snapping
noise. They chased me up trees only I could climb,
hitching myself up by my straps. Farm boys in big
tire pick-ups bumped us down the road. Bursts of
neon pointing the way. Jets of light, out along the
strip, shooting dots and arrows, thunderbirds, lone
stars. And farther out the windblown fields, ranch
gates with cowheads along empty stretches, without
a break. In a great rocky landscape there was a car
sculpture, made of cars like ours stuck nose first in
the ground, like lightning bolts with tail fins up in the
air. Another time we joined some men around a fire
in a hole. We'd been sleeping in the car, wherever we
could park, shivering all night, moving on whenever
a light was shined on us, and we sighted cooking
smoke in a field, pulled out over a fallen wire fence,
and wedged in between some parked jeeps. There
were about ten men in flag-colored windbreakers,
with talkies and field glasses, scanning the dark and
taking snapshot pictures. Belted-in men waiting for
us. They saw me and couldn't turn us away. They
were roasting fat slabs of meat and sausages. Shouting
at each other as if they were deaf, the way people
did in the open country, with their booming voices.
We weren't hungry but we needed the warmth. And
Papa was having his tremors. He was so thin the
wind blew through him, and bearded, like a wizard
in his cape. They were amazed and questioned him
and tried to make out what he said. I helped with

some worldly-wise chatter, which amused them.
They wanted to know if we'd seen any bushmen.
They meant gypsy workers. I realized then they were
a patrol. Their guns belted, shotguns on racks in the
jeeps. But they didn't bother us, though Papa had
long lost or given away our face cards, in minutes
they were drinking and backslapping with him,
having a big laugh, while I ate sizzling scraps off a
spit, then all together they pissed into the burning
hole to put out the fire, like firemen with their hoses,
Papa's hose the biggest of all, and they sent us on our
way. On past miles of scrub, gnarled thorn bushes,
bristling cactus, dwarf palms sticking out their
thatches, stunted trees twisted in the wind. Crows
or vultures wheeling on high. Some big opening
ahead. An opportunity worth Papa's life and power.
There'd been long-distance calls. They sounded like
organ notes on the hand phone. I thought of him as
a high-flying bird, a great mountain climber. Out
there somewhere was work his size, his place in the
world. Meantime we stopped for odd jobs. There was
always something, in a strip or a shopping center. He
fixed leaks and lights, made tricky connections. He
could find his way in a blackout. An electric current
would go through him without harming him. Once
he replaced broken letters on a neon board. He
climbed scaffolding, giving out flashes. He washed
an outdoor movie screen, left it bright as a mirror,
you could see the sky in it. Whatever was needed.
He owned night and day. We could have stayed on
anywhere we wanted. Even places that didn't let us
in, like a diner that was hiring dishwashers. They
wouldn't take us, but we hung around the parking

lot, where they served cars through a window, and at closing time they left food out for us, in foam boxes. Papa didn't eat, but I had enough and saved the rest, I made it last for two days, and even threw some of it out before it spoiled. Other times I grabbed snacks in dollar stores. Being crippled, it was easy, people looked the other way, sometimes they just let me have things. Toys and candy, which I sold to kids in the street. So I had my own business. It helped us buy a powder Papa used to stay awake. He could sniff it over a flame or inject it with a needle he'd gotten from the bums. It made his eyes wide and bright. He said he didn't want to miss anything. And we'd be on our way again. I'd been having wild dreams. I woke up with seat belt welts. We were both feverish. Sometimes when he had his tremors he let me steer, seated on his lap. No one saw us through the tinted windows. I felt him holding my bones together when I was coming unhinged. His fingernails had grown long, like his beard. Once, on a hazy hot road, miles from everywhere, when I lost sight of where I was going, we drove off the shoulder and bumped along a stony field with cactus crosses. One of the cactuses had flowered, as if Mama was there, and Papa waved down some pigeons, blowing on his spirit whistle, grasped at them in the air, searching for messages in their claws and beaks, and finally caught one, slit its crop with a razor-sharp thumbnail, and sent it off, spurting blood.

Then one day the car sank under us and rolled over into the ditch, crumpling around us, we barely managed to climb out, Papa as shaken as I was, getting us back on our legs, but that didn't stop us. A roadside assistance van picked us up. Papa had gotten through to it somehow. We had our belongings in a plastic bag: my straps and other devices, dollar store loot, trinkets for inventions, and grooming things, washcloths and paper towels to use in the bush, a shard of glass with which Papa chopped and trimmed his beard, also looking at himself in it, since it was a piece of mirror, Mama's beauty kit which we'd kept so I could paint on colors, everything, we didn't need emergency aid, just transportation. Papa kept telling the driver where to go. They held him in a back seat, but he knew the way. We ended up in a shelter called the Mansion House. A sort of converted hotel with drafty rooms, tall fans in corridors with staircases down into a courtyard. A plaque over the entrance said it was one of the hundred best places of its kind in the country. So we moved in, Papa hunching out of the long sleeves in which they'd tied his arms behind his back. I'd lost my walker in the wreck. And they'd taken our plastic bag, and emptied Papa's cape of dangerous objects, all our worldly possessions gone, so we were free, just wandering souls, like the other people there. Transients and regulars, on long or short stays. Some we knew, from our times with the bums. Or we'd seen them talking to strangers in the street. Homesick people tearing at themselves, or just gazing into space. They talked to their ghosts, hid secrets in folds and body holes. A man had been in a war. His memories weighed on him like corpses. He kept saying that. Others were missing arms or legs but acted as if they had them, gestured and walked without them, stood in line in the cafeteria carrying trays. I heard them talking out loud or in their minds.

They all had something to say. They ate and slept on their feet. Lined up along a rope with holiday balloons floating on strings. Restless, always awake, so nothing could surprise them, walking in place, dozing off and snapping back, they had it down to a fine art. Some went through motions of what they were thinking. They listened as if to someone in the next room. Each with his own language and his own meaning and message. They laughed and who-whoed like owls. And they had their ideas. A big Indian wrapped in a blanket said he was from the people of the light, and that they were the only real people. Papa questioned them and they listened to my parrot talk. Attendants took us around. As careful with Papa as with me. They'd felt his brittle bones. I'd already felt them when I clung to him. They couldn't pull us apart. They were like hospital people but more respectful. Amazed at Papa, who refused to eat. As he'd done in jail once, till they let him go. Still standing tall. He bowed and was gracious to them. And motherly nurses hugged and babied me, patched up my cuts and scratches. An exercise lady got my limbs working when I had a cramp. She made me walk in my sling, up some steps. It was like when I sleepwalked. I seemed to be stepping into my own feet. Then a healer did a backbreaking grip on me. He had a system, from the old country, he said. He made my bones snap in their joints. I couldn't help being noticed. Papa had brightened my face up, with pinpricks of blood he drew from his fingertips, since we didn't have Mama's beauty kit anymore, and I wore a smart seat belt buckle on my harness. I looked pale and soulful in my beauty mask, like Mama.

They wanted me to perform. So I showed them some things: movements you couldn't do normally, you had to be out of your mind, not knowing you couldn't do them. It was the secret of Papa's great strength: being more than yourself, like when he lifted a load several times his weight, without a thought. I could almost turn myself inside out, and they believed in me. Then I remembered one of Mama's bird songs. About fate and the passion for life. I had only my parroty voice, but she was singing in me. They heard it, too, and it meant a lot to them. So we could have stayed. It was one of our places. A preacher came around in the evening. He gave out holy books, the kind you found in bedside drawers in motels. I chanted with him, in his language. He made me chew gum so I could mouth the sounds. Papa did hand-waving things. Everyone was entertained, it was like in our market days. But we had to keep going. A sleeper crept up to me that night in the cot I shared with Papa. He had a knife and said he was going to cut me loose. I couldn't wake Papa, who was sprawled out, his arms and legs dangling over the sides. In the morning he was feverish. He'd been shuddering all night, burning up. And suddenly he grabbed me by my straps and in a couple of leaps over sleeping bodies we were out the door, which had been left open for us, into the sunlight. We crossed some used car lots. Battered beauties of cars like ours. He hadn't recovered his cape, and he snatched a shiny sun foil out of a car and wrapped us in it. I had our money belt. We caught a wind up a leafblown street. A patrol car gave us a lift, anywhere we wanted to go, they said, when Papa started giving them directions, and dropped us in the open highway. From there it was a long hot walk, but we had our sunfoil. I carried it flapping overhead, riding on Papa's back. He was like one of those huge cart horses on the other side hauling incredible loads up dusty roads, rearing up when the cart collapsed under it. I hung on with all my bones.

We made our way into a smoky town, down the edge of a road invaded by scorched grass, to where the sidewalk began, and he let me off and walked me downtown holding me up under my arms. My legs kept giving in, but he said I'd make it. We broke through some unfriendly people, Mister Sams types, blocking the way, casually, sort of bumping into us, and making remarks. Papa told them I was going and he had to see me off. He was wearing the sunfoil, which beat silvery wings, hoisting me up by the arms every few steps, over cracked sidewalks, along clouded shop windows, burned out neon signs, gatherings of bums, kids on skateboards, but we were on higher ground, onward bound.

It was a steamy factory town with a rundown square, hot alleys, warehouses along a foamy river, and those dirty pigeons like garbage birds flying down from the bare treees. Some of the kids on skateboards, doing fancy flips, lured us down a side street. They'd caught on to Papa, they said they wanted to show us something. Ganging up, from behind us, too, they drove us across empty yards, weedy back lots. A wasteland we'd found in every town. Buildings like bones crumbling to dust in the desert air. I was kicking out my legs, Papa holding me up, half-carrying me when I lost my footing. I knew whatever it was, he'd make it happen. The kids

goaded and shoved us along back alleys to a car dump
with towers of junk, a great scrap metal monument,
out of some crash landing, made of everything
under the sky, torn-up wrecks, fenders, hubcaps,
tail fins, antennas tall as trees, gleaming marvels of
things, like sunrays, firebirds. Ear-blasting motors
that were still alive made a pounding music. The
razor-sharp air buzzed, wired into radio sounds, lines
out in every direction, maybe even across the border.
The smashed cars with their ripped-out guts still
throbbing. And it was all Papa's doing. There was
a grandness and gallantry in the way he presented it
to me, as if calling it up from underground. Our car
might be there somewhere, dragged in from the road,
with its dashboard fan still going. There were beehive
radiators, torn hoods, shocks, springs, mufflers,
windshields, leaky batteries, their fumes poisoning
us, spares from wrecks for resale, like body parts.
The kids slept in tires and upholstery, a gutted trailer.
Ordinary kids who'd become street kids, I'd seen them
in the runaway houses with crazy haircuts, piercings
and tattoos. They welcomed us in silent awe. Hell
kids with hot metal burns and scabs, they drank from
oil cans. And Papa spat out a flame of firewater. He'd
been swallowing it and breathing it for days. Brittle
and dried out from not eating, a specter of himself.
Dusty as a ghost, shadowy under his skin. It was the
bruising, from our accident, coming up from deep in
his bones. Lost in his vision, with sunken eyes, when
the kids grabbed me, he handed me over. Shattered
when I was torn from him—but into something
big, he saw it. They were working on a burned-out
tailpipe, making it into a rocket, to shoot into space,

like a fiesta firecracker. A life machine he might have invented, with a time capsule to be opened in another world. They showed us the message it was carrying: drawings of a boy and a girl, stick figures, but one with breasts, the other with balls, to picture human life on earth. They needed samples, boy and girl bones, they said, and I had both, and Papa had arranged it and put everything he was into it and all the hopes he'd ever had for me. They made me drink and smoke hand rolled stubs of what tasted like metal dust. Puffs of foam drifted in from the river. There were flurries of pigeons. The kids shot at them with a blowtorch. And then suddenly they turned the torch on Papa. He was having his tremors, as if getting ready to fly, things dropping out of his sunfoil, he'd managed to scratch little pockets in it with his nails and stash them with the same things he'd had in his cape for his magic tricks, papers and bits of string and drugstore straws he'd been using for whistles, and he caught some shreds in the air, flicked his fingers and made a spiderweb that floated over us, almost gone into thin air, and the kids gaped and wondered at him, and that was when his hair caught fire. I was hanging by my straps from a winch, jumping up and down like a jumping jack, doing my boy-girl act, sucking myself in and letting myself out again, and somehow I wriggled free, and the kids, who hadn't known who we were, took fright and ran off, in a mad scramble, and enveloped in Papa's smoke and ashes, I crawled under a wire fence, through a drainage pipe that came out in the ditch scross the road. There were other body-size pipes along the ditch, with cracks in between, where they hadn't been joined yet, for miles, and I got through them, thrashing and banging my head on the walls, like when I had fits in my sleep, buried inside myself, and climbed out a hole in a field, in a wash of dirt and steaming dung.

Then Papa came for me. Up the highway, in a tremendous bucking and blasting life machine he'd gotten started, with banging doors, thumping tires, a hood like clapping jaws, all its junk parts fallen into place. It landed on me like a helicopter, pulled me up inside, and we took off, tailfires burning, blades whirling, chopping up the air, and taking signals. Papa wore a paint mask, like a motel Indian face: charcoal eyes and black finger streaks. He'd worn it before at a carnival, with head feathers and a beak, on some kind of Indian day. Now it was just the mask, and it was peeling off, in raw strips, but he drew his spiderweb cape, the net of ash that was left of his sunfoil, over it, and gripped the wheel with hands in rough gloves like claws. He didn't want to show himself at first, we filled up at a self-service pump he'd figured out, with clicking numbers, where he paid with a card I'd never known he had. But at the next stop, a dollar store where we went for equipment, he burst through the automatic door carrying me in a shopping cart we'd found in the parking lot. We bought canvas straps he picked out carefully and a parasol with a ballooning canopy, for some new exercise he'd devised for me. He'd thought of everything. We paid cash, with bills he'd gotten from a machine that gave out money. We were such a sight that no one looked at us. Half the bills scattered over the floor. We left without waiting for change. We had no time to waste. The car was boiling outside, blowing fireballs. In a minute, as we fitted ourselves into its bones, it took on our shape. We stepped on the speed, guzzling up miles, with our great wounded force and purpose. Papa's eyes oozing, as if his pupils were melting. I could still smell smoke on his breath. He had to stop a couple of times to vomit blood out the door. But by then we were going on some kind of wind or sun energy Papa said was faster than gas. Distances coming at us, birds blowing like smoke across the sky.

We rode through flat hot towns, razed by desert winds. In places a sort of dusty dry rain fell. The sun was like a pale moon in the distance. A burned-out back country Papa knew, like the inland ocean he'd told me about. He'd been there in his wanderings. Dead-end rails, junkyards, car dumps, empty motels with their VACANCY signs. One of those other worlds of his, where the messenger pigeons came from. Out on the open road, past crossroads midway between two nowheres named in blurred signs. An older, lost world in this one. Abandoned stretches of highway, dry river beds, a sandy waste where there'd been a cattle range. The great shapes under things, bigger and deeper than the ones you saw. A shadow world next to the ordinary world, mixed in with it. Papa had always known that. Great ruins of ghost towns, gas pumps with trashed cars, rusty steel bridges, twisted wrecks of buildings where only a few tramps lived, squatters and wayfarers, maybe some bush people, from before human times, Mama used to believe in them. We tore through in our life machine. The road split under us in earthquake cracks. You could tell where there'd been some disaster: fire, lightning, a flood. Behind an old cow town with wagon ruts there was one of those roadside graveyards. The graves had been dug up, into mounds of rubble, one with a scarecrow cross, another with a headstone that was a longhorn skull. People were picking up relics, rags or bones or bits of soil. And they left presents, a wreath of hair, a cactus flower. There was a burial tree with names and dates carved on its peeling bark, and messages, hearts and hands nailed to it, and clothes like a body without bones hanging from a branch. Late in the night, when the people were gone, we went and lay for a while in Mama's grave, which we recognized because of the warmth still coming up from underground.

We hurried, back on the highway. I was in such pain, Papa had to get me somewhere. We watched for signs, clattering through noisy towns, caught in truck traffic, street fairs where we were a spectacle, blowing a loud horn that sounded like a music band, railroad crossings, long drags in slow motion, with grinding brakes. And we began to see some great sights: factory rivers with bright oil slicks or sweating foam and flames, as if the earth were boiling up in them, high windows like movie screens with drifts of clouds, hot steam and ashes flying out chimneys. Down the main street, in low gear, gathering energy, we'd break through and out into the electric night with its golden arches, firebird motels, Big Mac palaces, lone star gas stations and others with wingspreads of roofs, starbursts overhead, zig-zag arrows like lightning, neon orbits spinning around each other, running lights spelling out messages, saucers scanning space for sounds, sky domes and needles, flying ramps and overpasses leading everywhere.

We came crashdriving into a town. In a gear-clashing commotion of old pick-ups with overheated motors and junkers with tail fins, like the one we used to have. Home-made motorcarts, plank shacks on hitches, with canvas tops. All of them piling into the windy hollows of a parking palace several stories high, a Lady Liberty building. Up ramps or lifted in a slow-moving cargo elevator, backing and maneuvering into pigeon holes with ticking meters that whirred when you dropped a coin in like a tin wish. We'd been expecting some such event. There'd been a moon day, with the sun half blotted out at noon. Papa wore his dollar store Indian beak and feathers and he'd outfitted me in the canvas straps and the ballooning canopy we'd bought for my new exercise, he said it was a parachute. We rose with the tide of cars. A coughing, smoking uproar. And, mixed in with it, a noisy flurry and what sounded like bird cries. I thought it was the coin meters whirring and screeching. But it was a bird market that had taken over the whole building. The rickety trucks in the parking slots were unveiling cages, bottle crates, wire mesh roosts, clothes trees with nests and hangers. We were swept into a feathery blur. Greeted by smugglers and performers with show birds. Our windows wide open to them. And it wasn't just the captive birds, there was an invasion of street birds that flew in from roof ledges, power lines. Barn swallows, starlings off high wires and billboards. Called in by caller birds. Pigeons too, making their flap, down from the girders. We had to wave them away. In slow motion, we visited birds in rings and cages. I met them with my talk and flutter. The crowd made way for us. They

sold the birds straight out of the trucks, to customers
of all sorts, Mister Sams traders with loud cars that
broke through the traffic jam, or furtive bag men who
ran with their catch down a back staircase into an
alley. Toy birds and decoys attracted attention. Paper
dragons like the ones Papa used to make. There were
reflecting mirrors and magnifying lenses where the
birds saw themselves in flashes of light and sang to
their image. Birds with gorgeous plumages, crests,
fantails, throaty warblers, and talking parrots that I
chatted with. I recognized the blind birds that didn't
fly out of their open cages or off their perches, just
stood there singing in an endless stream like trapped
spirits, their songs torn from them, spasms shooting
through their quivery nerves. And the hooded birds
waiting to be uncovered. Breasty beauties puffing
up. Butterfly birds that changed colors. Show birds
that flitted around on strings. Kids stood outstretched
like trees for them to land on their branches. It was
a big complicated set-up. Hidden birds were sold
underhand, others could be heard on recordings
played on gramophones and ordered. Birds caught
other birds' songs. They learned from each other,
Papa said. Embroideries, trills, runs, whistles. He
knew them all, I'd heard them on his bone flutes.
Soaring little soul birds and sad birds strung together,
in pairs or sets, and hung by the legs from racks and
wires. Almada birds and Bandera one -or four- legged
birds. Exotic birds and strange matches. There was a
laughing bird, another one looked like a flying fish, all
making their display. They stormed around bird baths
and feeders or hovered in mid-air. Feathery fountains
of light and a crazy joy. Love birds eating from each

other's craws. And those blind birds that sang their hearts out, a needle stuck through an eye into their brain. Like Mama's birds of sleep. I heard them in a silence behind the noise. Running on, streams of warbles. The visiting birds from the streets flitting in our windows. The birdmen and their customers dealt and bargained. Gawkers and buyers took calls on hand sets. They ushered us into every free slot we passed, but we didn't stay, just long enough to accept an offering. A mad bird beat on our windshield, then hopped and pecked on the glass, plucking out its neck and chest feathers, and nailed its beak to the hood. And they let me hold a baby bird fluttering in my hand. A shivery little bundle of live energy, its quiver went through me. In a heartbeat it gathered its brittle bones and was off. But other birds, flapping around wildly, had accidents, smashing into the walls. And there were sick birds, and I saw a manazas grab a suffering bird in his fist, break its neck with his thumb and cast off the crushed body. He was coming for me, but an alarm saved me, police sirens, a raid, trampling steps, up the ramps and out the elevator. The birds were set free: a frenzy of wings in every direction. Even the ones hanging with folded wings like bats whooshed out into the alleys and holes of other buildings. Some that wouldn't or couldn't fly the men set fire to and sent off in flames that crumbled into ashes, with the ghosts of twitchy bones still visible. Manazas and Mister Sams ran the show. But Papa, smoldering in his beak and feathers, was the big birdman who made it all happen. By then we were all the way up and out on the flat roof, where the flashing Lady Liberty sign was, our life machine going fast, and the great inspiring haze of the world surrounding us, Papa's vast inland sea with its reflections of distant things, and the messenger pigeons flying out there, and I was wearing my parachute, and Papa blowing his spirit whistle, we drove off the edge, into the upside down images rising toward us out of the deep.

I sank way down, in shady waters, but I could swim, so I came back up to the surface, in easy strokes, breaking out of my body, like in my dreams, and as Papa had taught me to do, my loose bones floating around me. On my back, arms and legs rippling, I basked weightless in the sun. Shafts of light and life going through me. Then some Bonita kids pulled me ashore. They'd seen me coming out of myself. Pony kids on their shaggy mounts with bushy tails. Probably the Rico Chico gang with their swimming ponies. We'd met them working in fairs renting out rides and doing stunts on the ponies, flips, handsprings. Managed by their Mesias who stayed out of sight, but with an almighty power over them. Bought and sold many times. Photo kids, too, who posed for pictures. Angels and devils in pageants. Others with grown-up beauties to show. Joy girls and love boys. They knew who I was, writhing in their hands. A feverish last fire in me. A busty Maria girl and a throbbing love boy milk-fed me. At night they kept me wrapped into them, their hands on me, feeling my body change shapes, hips and ribs sticking out, unexpected growths and hot spots, feeding me out of their mouths, their tongues inside me. And in the morning they slung me across a broad-bottomed horse, like Bravo the boat horse that did river crossings from the other side. A special horse, squat as the ponies but with a jaunty swing in its stride, and a deepset power in its bones, as I settled comfortably into the dip of its sway back. So we set out, making big flops. In a blazing sun, wearing donkey hats, swishing off flies. Packs of muscle moving the huge girth I straddled, a great underforce. We went snorting with energy, breaking into sudden starts and joys, pissing in loud squirts. The kids alongside me on their uppity mounts. They urged them on with tongue clicks and chirrups, strutting along in cowboy chaps and hats, digging starball spurs into their sides and flicking rawhide switches. Freaky ponies, some of them, strange crossbreeds, with knotty bones, humps, donkey danglers, udders, hairy fetlocks like wings, horns, sores where the brands of the ranches from which they'd been stolen had been burned off. An old bearded pony that tagged along was like a sacred beast, no one rode it. There were extra ponies in a train, a love pony that was mounted by other ponies. They saw at night, following a lead pony that wore a headlight, and went on walking asleep in their skins, stomping and knocking shoulders. The kids said their Mesias was waiting for us. But I knew it was Papa.